ARIZONA GUN LAW

J.T. Edson

ARIZONA GUN LAW

WHEELER
PUBLISHING, INC.
ROCKLAND, MA

★ AN AMERICAN COMPANY ★

Published in Large Print by arrangement with Dell Publishing, a division of Bantam Doubleday Dell Publishing Group, Inc. in the United States and Canada

Wheeler Large Print Book Series.

Set in 16 pt Plantin.

Library of Congress Cataloging-in-Publication Data

Edson, J. T.
   Arizona gun law / J.T. Edson.
      p. (large print) cm.(Wheeler large print book series)
   ISBN 1-56895-483-2 (softcover)
   1. Large type books. I. Title. II. Series
[PR6055D8A87 1997]
823'.914—dc21

97-30640
CIP

Dedicated by Tiberius the Tarantula and myself to our favorite ornithologist, student of the "Boid," Wild Turkey that is, and teller of risque jokes, Halina Maj.

AUTHOR'S NOTE

While complete in itself, this narrative follows immediately after the events recorded in WEDGE GOES HOME and ARIZONA RANGE WAR.

When supplying us with the information from which we produce our books, one of the strictest rules imposed upon us by the present-day members of what we call the "Hardin, Fog, and Blaze" clan and the "Counter" family is that we never under any circumstances disclose their true identity or present locations. Furthermore, we are instructed to always employ enough inconsistencies with regard to periods and places in which incidents take place to ensure that neither can happen even inadvertently.

We would also point out that the names of people who appear in this volume are those supplied to us by our informants in Texas, and any resemblance with those of other persons, living or dead, is purely coincidental.

To save our old hands repetition, but for the benefit of new readers, we have given "potted biographies" of Captain Dustine Edward Marsden "Dusty" Fog, Mark Counter, and the Ysabel Kid in the form of Appendixes.

We realize that, in our present permissive society, we could use the actual profanities employed by various people in the narrative.

However, we do not concede that a spurious desire to create realism is any justification for doing so.

Since we refuse to pander to the current trendy usage of the metric system, except when referring to the caliber of certain firearms traditionally measured in millimeters—e.g., Luger 9mm—we will continue to employ miles, yards, feet, inches, pounds and ounces when quoting distances and weights.

Lastly, and of the greatest importance, we must stress that the attitudes and speech of the characters is put down as would have been the case at the period of this narrative.

J.T. Edson
Melton Mowbray
Leics.,
England

ARIZONA GUN LAW

1

SO YOU AIM TO KEEP ON WITH IT?

"I've never had so much *lousy* luck!" Anthony Blair stated in a whining voice that even after many years in the United States had an accent that still gave evidence he had grown up in Birmingham, England. "*Everything's* gone wrong."

"Not quite everything," Willis Norman objected in his surly New England tones. "At *least* Jack Straw made sure that lousy, yellow-bellied Nicholson couldn't tell any more than he already had about what we had him do."

"It should have been done a damned sight *sooner!*" Graeme Steel pointed out, although he hated to have to give even a suggestion that another of the men he had been responsible for hiring had proved wanting in any way. Bitter in timbre, his voice gave no indication of his origins in its accent and manner. "The bastard gave them *my* name before he died."

"That was *bad* luck," Norman admitted, but without any noticeable sympathy over such information having been supplied, since his name had not been included in it as far as he knew.

"*Real* bad, for *you,* Steel, I'll admit," Blair went on, also without any concern over what had been told to the men who had captured and were compelling John Nicholson—the senior land agent for Arizona Territory—to tell them

1

certain things that he and his companions had no desire to be disclosed. The reason for the lack of commiseration was the same as that of the previous speaker. "At least Straw got us out of the Spreckley so we could come here, where nobody knows how to find us, before either those two ranchers from Spanish Grant County who the half-breeds are working for, or the law if they've reported the killing, could come to see us about it."

Although the three men seated around the table in the small yet well-furnished room had been partners for some time in a scheme by which they hoped to make a fortune apiece and gain positions of great power in Arizona, there was a marked contrast in their respective physical appearances.

Small, lean, and with parchmentlike sharp features, Blair looked as if he were a not too successful undertaker even when he had been occupying the best suite offered by the Spreckley Hotel in Prescott, from which he and the other two had been advised earlier in the evening to take a hurried departure. Elsewhere throughout Arizona, the most noticeable thing about him would have been that there was no sign of his being armed. However, this was no particularly noticeable omission in the capital of Arizona, which remained a territory and had not been raised to the state many people—but not he and his associates, at least not until they were able to exert a considerable control over its affairs—hoped to have it become.[1]

1. Phoenix did not become the capital city of Arizona until after 1889.

Capable of producing an aura of convincing and reassuring bonhomie when it was required, which he did not think was the case at that moment, Norman was close to seven inches taller than Blair and weighed nearly twice as much. Massive of lines and porcine of face, on less stressful occasions he could present a friendly demeanor implying he was far more trustworthy than was really the case. His bulky body strained at the costly Eastern garments he wore; he, too, gave no indication of bearing weapons of any kind on his person. Under normal conditions, it was his part in their partnership to provide an amicable atmosphere leading to trust or cooperation on the part of the one being subjected to it, which neither of the others was suited by appearance or nature to deliver no matter how great the need.

In many respects, Steel was a much less noticeable figure than either of his two associates. He was in height and build between them, and everything about him—even his city-style clothing—was so ordinary in appearance that he could easily have passed unnoticed through a crowd at any level of Prescott society, except where those, such as cowhands, who wore attire peculiar to their specific line of work were concerned. He had mouse-brown hair—now left visible by the plain gray derby hat he was carrying—and a face devoid of characteristics. Despite being equally wealthy and unscrupulous, he seemed to have nothing in common with his associates. Nevertheless, like them, he possessed a number of contacts of vital importance, and one of them accompanied him now.

Having spent most of their grown-up lives involved in various kinds of activities, not all of them legal, this diverse and unlikely trio of partners had been brought together with the intention of gaining possession of a large piece of land in Arizona. There had also been a side issue, which was even more illegal than the means they had elected to bring about the primary object: obtaining a large sum of money in a lump sum to add to their long-term profits.

Because Congress had ratified the Spanish grant for its original owner when the annexation of Arizona by the United States was completed on February 24, 1863, the vast area of land that became the county of that name remained under his control despite the envious eyes that were constantly being cast upon it by various American speculators eager to gain possession of it. His dominance had been far from despotic. In fact, he had allowed a town owned by American businessmen of various kinds to rise in the center of the area. When he died intestate and no members of his race put in claims, the government in Washington, D.C.—many members of which had never favored the proposition of one person, especially one with Mexican citizenship, owning so great an area on United States soil—had ruled that it would be divided into four equal portions demarcated by natural features such as hill ranges and rivers.

Hearing what was proposed through sources in the national capital before the matter was made public, Blair, Norman, and Steel had seen a way to eventually acquire the whole region.

4

They had known any attempt to bring this about as a single corporation would be resisted strenuously and probably be to no avail, so they had sought a man sufficiently ruthless to carry out the scheme. Having been acquainted with Eustace Edgar Eisteddfod under a different name in Washington, D.C., Norman had claimed that his knowing something of the reason for the change of identity made him perfect for their needs.[2] At the beginning, the alleged Welshman had carried out his duties to the complete satisfaction of his employers. He had selected the candidates for ownership of the other three ranches and made them agree to a contract drawn up by an attorney in Prescott whereby any who died let his land be shared between the survivors.

The trio had accepted from the start that a considerable amount of time would have to pass before the scheme came to fruition, and they had been required to take on some silent partners they would have preferred to avoid to help with the financing. Despite there having so far been no profit accruing in return for the considerable expenditure required, which the unwelcome backers had accepted as inevitable, the arrangements went along in a manner that met with the approval of the three conspirators. They had allowed a sufficient period to elapse for the quartet to become

2. The reason why the change in name to Eustace Edgar Eistteddfod—the latter name chosen as suggesting that the Welsh background was genuine, as the former alias had sought to indicate a Scottish birthright—was made is told in TEXAS KIDNAPPERS.

accepted as bona fide landowners, even though only Cornelius MacLaine had had experience of the cattle business and the other three would be dependent on the honest foremen who were obtained to carry out the running of the ranches. The conspirators—having continued their less-than-honest speculations elsewhere to maintain their finances—had gathered in Prescott to keep a watchful eye on developments from closer at hand. With the assistance of an agent based in Child City, the seat of Spanish Grant County, they had instructed Eisteddfod to commence the next stage of the scheme.

With the aid of an ex-jockey called Beagle who had been barred from his employment in that line for dishonesty, the "Welshman" had arranged for Douglas Loxley of the Lazy Scissors ranch to die by what appeared to be a riding accident. Too late it had been discovered that the ranch had been left in an incontestable will to a kinsman, Major Wilson Eardle, who had recently retired after a career with the United States Cavalry. To make matters worse, when a similar fate befell MacLaine, who ran the CM brand, it was discovered that he too had arranged for the property to go to a relative, a Texan called Jethro "Stone" Hart, well-known for running a group of very competent and loyal contract trail drivers known as the Wedge. The three conspirators had decided that Hart, more experienced in all matters pertaining to the cattle business and the ways of the West, could prove much the tougher nut to crack.

Eisteddfod had suggested what might be done

to make their scheme successful. After receiving the backing they required, including a group of young Easterners donated by some of the wealthy liberals in Washington, D.C.— who had no desire to see Arizona attain statehood unless they could gain at least some control of its legislature—the Welshman had set about trying to create hostility between the two new ranch owners and stir up animosity against both in Child City. There had followed a series of failures that ended with Eisteddfod, Beagle, and the leader of the hired guns who were supplied by the conspirators dead, fortunately without any of them being able to tell what had brought them to their fate.

With much money already invested in the scheme, despite having found that the liberals were disinclined to supply more financial aid, the conspirators had no intentions of giving up their efforts. However, they had already acquired more lucrative backing, so this had not worried them unduly. Although they had failed to acquire the services of Hayden Paul Lindrick, the only professional gunfighter who would be suitable for a scheme to have the bank in Child City robbed and bring about the ruin of many of the local citizens, they had discovered that the robbery had been attempted anyway. According to information they had received, the attempt had ended in failure.[3]

3. Why the man then using the name Hayden Paul Lindrick— he had once used another name—had declined the offer is explained in DOC LEROY, M.D

7

The bad luck to which Blair had referred had continued.

Instead of having been provoked into starting a range war between them, the men who had inherited two ranches made vacant by the murder of the previous owners had settled their differences amicably and become friends. Nor had this been changed by two ideas for creating discord between them and the citizens of Child City, instigated by the conspirators.

Guessing correctly that Stone Hart and Major Wilson Eardle—who had changed the brands of their respective properties to the Wedge and AW—would try to purchase one of the other two ranches that became available through the death of the surviving pair involved in the plot, the trio had sought to prevent them from reaching the office of the territorial land agent and making a bid by having them ambushed and killed on the journey between Child City and Prescott.[4] Even though this had failed, fortunately with the only one involved who might have led the law to the conspirators having died in the ensuing fighting, they had set in motion another plot. By a combination of bribery and blackmail, they had induced John Nicholson to accept forged documents claiming that the dead ranchers had also left their properties to kinsmen.

Satisfied that they had done all they could to protect their interests from the ranchers,

4. Illustrations of the various brands for ranches in Spanish Grant County referred to in the narrative are given in WEDGE GOES TO ARIZONA.

the trio had received a message by telegraph in code from their informant in Child City. The bank robbery had failed, again with the only person who could have betrayed them killed in the attempt. However, the misfortunes had not ended there. Waylaid while on his way to visit a prostitute in one of the town's houses of ill repute, this married man and pillar of the community had been induced by his captors to start telling things they would not have wished to be disclosed. He had been killed by one of the men they had hired, but not before he had revealed Steel's name and their location. Warned of this by the man, they had left the hotel and taken advantage of an offer from an associate to make use of his home while he and his wife were away on vacation.

"Maybe *you* should go east as soon as you can," Norman suggested, eyeing the undistinguished-looking man in a pointed fashion.

"Like hell I will," Steel refused determinedly.

"Only until things quieten down," Blair suggested.

"You're not getting rid of me that easily!" Steel snarled. He was suspicious by nature and had no faith in the integrity of the men with whom he was cooperating. "We're all in this together, and that's the way it's going to stay."

Before the partners could continue what appeared likely to develop into another of their frequently acrimonious debates—none was willing to accept any assumption of leadership by the others or to accept blame for anything that went amiss—the door of the room was opened without the formality of a knock.

The man who came unbidden across the threshold carried a well-worn, tan-colored J. B. Stetson hat with its crown taken up into a Montana peak.[5] The trio recognized him immediately as Jack Straw. Despite the politeness implied by the way he entered, there was nothing subservient in his attitude. Rather, he looked as though he considered himself to be on terms of equality with those he had come to see. Because of the reason they had originally made contact with him, and because he already knew about their plans, they had to admit—if only each to himself—that this was close to being the case.

Straw's brown hair was short-cropped and going gray at the temples, and his heavily mustached tanned face had the texture of old leather. His attire was the functional working garb of a cowhand from the state that supplied the name for his headdress style. Well-made, his gunbelt carried a brace of walnut-handled Colt Model P of 1873 Peacemaker revolvers. The one at the right was a Civilian Model and hung just right for a rapid withdrawal. However, with its handle turned forward to allow a draw with either hand, the one on his left was a longer Cavalry Model that allowed for more accurate shooting over great distances, as he had proved earlier that night when killing Nicholson. He advanced with a leisurely-seeming yet swift stride, and

5. "Montana peak": having the crown adapted in the fashion of the hats that used to be part of the uniform for Boy Scouts.

10

although his boots—which had the pointed toes but lacked the high heels of those worn by members of the trade—themselves made no sound, the big spurs attached to their heels gave a noticeable jingling that had necessitated their removal before he moved into firing position earlier that night.

"Mind if I help myself to a drink 'n' a smoke, gents?" the newcomer inquired and, after receiving a nod from Steel, went to get the required items from the top of the sidepiece. Having taken a glass half full of whiskey and a cigar, he returned to the table. "Well, none of 'em's gone to see the town clown or the sheriff so far, them both using the same building. 'Course, they could have put what they know in the hands of the Pink-Eyes, seeing as how that's where they went after leaving the land agent's."

"Didn't you follow them to see if they did?" Norman growled.

"*Mister,*" Straw said quietly. "I concluded I'd already got away with more'n I was rightly calculated to expect dogging the Ysabel Kid 'n' Kiowa Cotton the *one* time. I sure as shit wasn't fixing to try for seconds. Which being, I drifted around to where I could keep an eye on the lawmen."

"Are those two half-breeds as *dangerous* as all that?" Steel inquired.

"If they *ain't,* I surely don't want to run up ag'in' anybody who *is,*" the hired gun replied. "Being dudes's've never needed to know how much *less* do such, you don't have no notion of just how lucky I was to make it out there in the piny woods 'n' come away walking. Anyways, what's doing now?"

"How do you mean?" Blair inquired. He was not one to be left out of any conversation in which his associates were taking part.

"This deal of your'n," Straw explained. "Do you aim to keep on with it?"

"We *do*," Steel asserted before either of the others could speak, but he refrained from saying that they had no other choice than to continue since their backers were not men likely to forget and forgive the money that had been invested in their scheme and were liable to have arranged very painful measures as a reprisal.

"Do you still need me?" the hired gun inquired in an indifferent fashion that suggested he was not particularly worried if the answer should be in the negative.

"I thought you were scared of those two half-breeds," Norman sneered, unable to resist a dig at Steel, who had been responsible for employing Straw and the other two hired guns, neither of whom had proved of assistance to the scheme.

"Mister," Straw answered quietly, but his whole bearing suddenly became charged with menace. "I'm not scared of *them* no more'n I'm scared of a winter-starved grizzly bear sow with newborn cubs, but I'd keep clear of *her* unless there wasn't no way of doing it. You feel that way about me, I can easy 'nough go someplace else."

"I don't feel that way!" Steel stated. He glowered at Norman, since he knew what had motivated the remark and had also read an implied threat in it.

12

"Or me," Blair seconded, equally aware that the leathery-faced hired gun knew enough of their affairs to be able to find a ready market for what he could tell.

"That just leaves *you*," Straw stated, his eyes having remained on the bulky man.

"Hell, I didn't mean anything by what I said," Norman claimed, though his voice lacked conviction. He, too, knew that Straw had a market for the information readily available in Prescott. "We want you to stay on."

"And do what?" the hired gun asked. "I'm not choosy most times, but there's a limit to how many risks I take compared with what I'm being paid."

"We'll want crews for the two ranches we'll have taken over," Steel explained.

"And you'll not want 'em to be saints like they are now?" Straw guessed. "Which means you don't want *honest* cowhands like I've heard is the case up to Spanish Grant."

"What we want," Blair supplemented to show that he was acquainted with some aspects of the West, "is the kind I've heard John Chisum calls 'warriors.' "[6]

"They'll not be overhard to come by," Straw assessed. "Given time."

"How much time?" Norman wanted to know.

"Hell, I can't say for sure," the hired gun admitted. "You don't get them kind a-swarming like bees around a honey pot, 'specially in Prescott, though I'll admit there could be a few.

6. Some information about John Chisum is given in FROM HIDE AND HORN *and Part One, "They Called Him the Cattle King,"* SLAUGHTER'S WAY.

I'll have to pass the word to fetch 'em in. With luck, I'll have enough for a working start in a couple of weeks. Unless that'll be too long."

"It might be just what we need," Steel declared. "There's no way even the Pinkertons can check up on the documents we gave to Nicholson sooner than that, if at all, and there's nothing Eardle and Hart can do to stop our men taking over the ranches until they know for sure what's happened. It could lull them into a sense of false security and, before they hear, we'll have them both crewed with our own men."

"Sounds like smart figuring to me," Straw claimed. "Have you anything else in mind until something blows?"

"We *have*," Steel confirmed. "And it could be we'll be needing you to help us bring off what we're going to have done."

"You'll get said help," Straw promised. "'Cepting we're going to have to do some hoss-trading over what I'm going to be paid."

"That's already been settled," Norman claimed, darting a less-than-amiable glance at Steel, who had made the financial arrangements without consulting either him or Blair.

"Only in a general way," the hired gun pointed out. "You're not dealing with a stupid yack like Taos Lightning, who got gunned down trying to take out Hart 'n' Eardle, gents. I know that, after so much has gone wrong for you already, you must have a damned powerful reason for wanting to go on."

"What would that be?" Blair wanted to know, as did the other two, since finding out would let them know how they stood.

14

"Arizona's still only a territory," Straw replied. "Only, it's already a-coming part of these here United States, having so much gold, silver, copper 'n' such. There's even talk about getting railroads coming through. All of which makes me reckon's how you gents ain't interested in getting hold of them ranches just to raise cattle." His ability as a poker player led him to believe that he was speaking the truth about the trio's motivation, so he continued, "Which being, gents, I con- clude I want more money'n I've been offered so far."

2
I'VE COME *ALONE*, LIKE YOU SAID I SHOULD

On the way to visit Matilda Canoga to inquire after the baby she had delivered in her capac- ity as a trained nurse, having arrived on an errand for Margaret Hart and April Eardle, Stephanie Willis—whose given name was usu- ally reduced to Steffie—saw the unmistakable figure of Miss Martha "Calamity Jane" Canary walking toward an area of woodland just beyond the edge of Child City.

Steffie, five feet five and in her mid-twenties, had her ash-blond hair drawn tightly into a bun at the back of her head as usual. She had slightly aquiline attractive features that conveyed a suggestion of a spirited nature that would be disinclined to allow any liberties to be taken with her. While the blue and white gingham dress she had on—the short sleeves left her sturdy arms exposed from the biceps down—was of the decorous cut required by a woman who qualified as "good" by the classifications of the West, its bodice and upper skirt fitted snugly enough to indicate that her close-to-buxom physical attributes were comprised of firm flesh and that the hourglass contours were natural, not produced by artificial aids from undergarments. The rest of her visible ensemble was black stockings and shoes with low heels.

She had decided to send word to her husband that she was in town, in the hope that they could spend a short while together before she had to return to the Wedge ranch—if he was not engaged on any urgent duty as temporary deputy sheriff. However, wanting to stretch her legs after having driven a buckboard into town, she set off after the girl instead of calling out.

Five feet seven in height and only just over twenty, Calamity Jane was a sight most men would have considered comely as she walked along in the warmth of the early afternoon. Beneath a dark-blue and well-worn U.S. Cavalry kepi perched at a jaunty angle on a mop of shortish curly red hair, she had a face that was merely pleasing to look upon rather than outstandingly beautiful. Tanned and sprinkled with freckles that added to its charm, it had sparkling blue eyes, a slightly snub nose, and a mouth that looked made for laughing or kissing. As was usually the case, she was dressed in a decidedly unconventional fashion.

Possessed of a full and firm figure, the redhead had it displayed to its best advantage by a man's tartan shirt whose neck was open lower than could be considered decorous. In addition to conforming to the contours of her bosom, over the left dome of which was pinned the badge of a deputy sheriff, the shirt revealed the top of a red woolen undershirt in the deep V formed by its neckline. Her multihued and tightly rolled bandanna trailed its long ends downward over her torso. Like the garment tucked into its waistband, her Levi's pants—the legs with cuffs almost three inches in depth and showing just a trace of white woolen socks ending in Indian moccasins—appeared to have been bought a trifle too small and further shrunk by washing, judging from the way they conformed to her well-rounded hips and buttocks.

Slanting down from Calamity's right hip, a well-designed gunbelt carried an ivory-handled Colt Model of 1851 Navy revolver—which had the Thuer conversion to allow it to accept .36-caliber metallic case bullets, thus obviating the need for separate percussion cap, powder, and ball—with the butt turned forward in its low-tied holster. On the left side was a wide leather loop into which was tucked the handle of a coiled long-lashed bullwhip made specially lightweight to suit her physical development, but no less effective on that account. Anybody who knew her well could have stated that, like the gun, the whip was no mere decoration. On more than one occasion during her hectic young life, she had proved herself competent at using each.

While walking, Calamity found herself amused by the turn of fate that caused her to be doing so. When her boss, Cecil "Dobe" Killem, had sent her with other of his freight-wagon drivers to transport Derek Hatton, Steven Scott, their male employees, and property to Child City, she had not expected to once again be brought into contact with the Texans who were the most prominent members of the floating outfit for General Jackson Baines "Ole Devil" Hardin's OD Connected ranch. She had known them all, especially Mark Counter, for some time and had pleasant memories of all their meetings, even though some of these encounters had proved fraught with danger. Nor had she anticipated that their leader, Captain Dustine Edward Marsden "Dusty" Fog—the rank had been given to him in the Army of the Confederate States during the Civil War—would ask her in his capacity as temporary sheriff of Spanish Grant County to serve as a deputy.[1] It was the first time she had worn the badge of a peace officer, and she was finding doing so to be a stimulating and interesting experience.

Unaware that she was being followed at a distance by the ash-blonde, Calamity was wondering what information might be awaiting her as she entered the area of woodland to which the note—written in a sprawling feminine hand and shoved under the door of her room at the Summers Hotel—said she must come alone, since it was a matter for a woman's ears only. She suspected that Dusty

1. Information regarding the military career of Captain Dustine Edward Marsden "Dusty" Fog, along with his family background and special qualifications, is given in Appendix One.

Fog would not approve of her setting off without at least letting him know she intended to do so. He had insisted upon enlisting her aid when asked to take over as sheriff of Spanish Grant County as an interim replacement for Amon Reeves, who had been badly wounded in the attempt to rob the Cattlemen's Bank.[2]

However, the redhead drew consolation from the thought that Dusty was occupied with Counselor Edward Sutherland, justice of the peace for the area and therefore devoted to problems arising from the prevention of the crime. What was more, even if she had wanted to have one or both of them accompany her in defiance of the instructions she received, the two male deputies were needed for other tasks. Thorny Bush was busy guarding the survivor of the robbers, and Rusty Willis was patrolling the town watching for any suggestion that its population might be contemplating unofficial justice against him because of his part in the murder of Toby Canoga, who had been a popular member of the community.

Therefore, being the kind of self-reliant person she was, Calamity had decided to follow the instructions by coming unattended. She had concluded that she could claim she simply felt justified in acting on her own initiative in following up on something that

2. The conspirators had intended that Hayden Paul Lindrick would be in Child City to volunteer his services as temporary sheriff after the wounding of Amon Reeves. He was to ensure that the bank robbery was successful by the way he handled its aftermath.

might prove of importance. The real reason was that, having a fair share of curiosity and the love of adventure that made her the woman she was, she could not resist going alone on anything she found intriguing. If there should prove to be a sinister motive behind the note, although she was unable to imagine what it might be, she had confidence in her ability to deal with anything that came up.

Entering a clearing that she had been told she would find by following a narrow track, Calamity decided she had indeed walked into a trap!

Although their footwear was the kind they would wear when working, the garments worn by the six women who stood looking at the redhead in a calculating and distinctly hostile fashion were clearly the oldest garments each possessed. Even if the redhead did not recognize them as female employees for the old cantina that two men with whom she had had trouble shortly after arriving at Child City intended to reopen for business, she would have known they were workers in a saloon. That showed in their hairstyles and in their heavily made-up faces. However, while none was wearing jewelry of any kind, they all had on elbow-length gloves of different types of fabric. They were of various ages and different heights, and they had builds ranging from slender to buxom, the largest being of dimensions exceeding those of Calamity. None of them, even the most slender, struck the redhead as being puny, and the Junoesque silvery-blonde who was clearly the ringleader was bulky and clearly more than passably strong.

"All right," Calamity said. She halted as

soon as she saw the women and stood on spread-apart feet, with her right hand turning palm out close to the butt of the Navy Colt, yet also ready to cross to the handle of the bullwhip, which she knew she could produce and use with considerable alacrity. "I've come alone, like you said I should. So what do you want to tell me?"

"That you beat the hell out of my kid sister one night in a saloon when she was too liquored up to fight back," stated the largest of the group, a dyed-blonde in her mid-thirties who had a menacing demeanor. Driving her clenched left fist into the black-gloved palm of her right hand, she went on, "So I want to see how you stack up against somebody who is cold sober."

"That somebody being *you*?" Calamity inquired, although she knew what the answer was going to be.

"You're right on it," stated the youngest member of the party, a cheerful-looking rusty-brunette with a rubbery buxom build. "Winnie's been waiting for a chance ever since we saw you were in town."

"Doxie's never said a truer word," declared the willowy grizzled-brunette at the left side of the circle of women. Her accent had a more Irish than French timbre despite her name, and her footwear was the kind used by ballet dancers, except that the toes were not constructed to allow extended periods on them. "And you can take the word of Fifi le Planchet when she gives it."

"So what does *Winnie* aim to do, Doxie, Fifi, 'n' the rest of you?" the redhead asked in a mocking tone, watching every move and ready

21

to respond as she thought best suited to her needs. There was still enough distance between her and the group for the bullwhip to be brought into play, but the number of women she would be in contention with suggested that she might have to rely on the Colt as her means of protection. "Have you bunch hold me still while she works me over?"

"I'd say that's up to *you*," the big dyed-blonde declared, still slapping the fist into the palm. "You allus reckon to be so goddamned much tougher than anybody else, I reckoned I should give you a chance to prove it."

"You bunch know I'm one of Cap'n Dusty Fog's deputies, don't you?" Calamity said quietly, and gestured with her left hand toward the badge of office fastened to the left breast of her shirt.

"We know you bed right regular with Mark Counter among a heap of others, given half a chance," Winnie Ashwell replied. She had been sent by Hatton and Scott to find an excuse to attack the redhead in revenge for the part she had played in causing a savage dog they owned to be killed. They were to provoke a response that would allow Winnie to claim she did so in self-defense as her companions would testify had been the case when questioned by the local peace officers.[3] She had also been told to avoid having the damage they inflicted be from heavy rings or raking fin-

---

3. The special relationship that existed between Miss Martha "Calamity Jane" Canary and Mark Counter of Ole Devil Hardin's floating outfit, Counter's family background, and other pertinent details are supplied in Appendix Two.

feared might prove to be the case—the conflict would not remain restricted to herself and Winnie. Seeing their friend in difficulty, Doxie began to move forward, followed by Fifi.

3
THIS IS *WORSE* THAN YOU GUESSED!

"Good heavens!" the medium-sized and less-than-slender owner of Clitheroe's General Emporium said, looking at the two men seated on the other side of the desk in the business office of the Cattlemen's Bank. He had been summoned by Counselor Edward Sutherland—who had given the usual kind of mock dour warning that no fee could be expected for the service in behalf of Spanish Grant County—to carry out an inspection of the books kept by Robin C. Harman, who had had charge of the establishment before being killed in the thwarted robbery. Having just completed enough of an inspection to form an opinion, he spoke in a worried tone that matched the expression now on his normally amiable face. "You were right to call me in, Scot—Judge."

"Not yet, Amos, not *yet,*" the attorney corrected in his Bostonian voice, which carried a trace of a Scottish burr. His sun-reddened face bore an ingenuous cast that had caused more than one opponent in a court case to think him a soft touch before being most effectively disillusioned. He was not much taller than the storekeeper and was endowed with a similarly well-padded build, although in his case the padding was hard flesh and muscle, the result of regular indulgence in strenuous outdoor activities. "I'm merely here in my capacity of *unpaid* justice of the peace for the county. Captain Fog and I considered it advisable to call upon your services—without you having the expectancy of a consultation fee—as neither of us are what you might term experts at bookkeeping."

"And you were wise to do it," Clitheroe declared, smiling despite his concern at the invariable way in which his old friend played the part of the parsimonious stereotypical Scot. He was aware that, although the lawyer was granted a percentage of all fines imposed in the local court, the generally law-abiding state of the town under Sheriff Amon Reeves meant that the sum total was far from munificent. The reference to the lack of an appearance fee stemmed from Sutherland's habit of claiming one—in the form of a drink of whiskey, or a cigar—whenever he was called upon for an opinion that might be termed legalistic in nature. However, the merriment disappeared and he continued somberly, "This is *worse* than you guessed!"

Unaware that the female deputy he had appointed had without informing him gone on a mission that even now was putting her in a serious predicament—although he would not have been surprised to learn of what she was doing, knowing her as well as he did—Dusty Fog sat in a seemingly relaxed fashion as he listened to the storekeeper speak.

There was nothing in Dusty's outward mien to suggest how he had already attained considerable acclaim in several fields of endeavor peculiar to the West despite still being in his mid-twenties. He was only five feet six in his high-heeled, sharp-toed brown Justin boots and his Texas-style black J. B. Stetson hat, now hanging by its *barbiquejo* chin strap on the rack by the door of the office. His neatly trimmed hair was a dusty-blond color. He was moderately good-looking at first sight about his tanned face; however, a closer examination revealed a strength of will and intelligence in its lines. There was a spread to his shoulders that trimmed down at the waist and would have hinted at above-average strength if it had been noticeable when he was in apparent repose. His clothing was that of a working cowhand and was of excellent quality, but because they concealed his Herculean physique, they had the appearance of being castoffs from somebody better favored in height and built. Nor did the gunbelt he had on, with twin bone-handled Colt Civilian Model Peacemaker revolvers butt forward in cross-draw holsters, make him seem impressive.

"I must admit there was less money in the cellar than I would have expected, considering how many depositors there are," Sutherland said quietly. "That must be why the Harmans tried to make things look like there'd been a robbery."

"Why, sure," Dusty agreed, his voice the lazy drawl of a well-educated Texan. "She gunned the sheriff down, figuring there wouldn't be time for you to send for somebody to replace him until he's well again."

"Only, I was able to bring *you* in as soon as

I heard what had happened," the attorney went on. "But surely they'd have known that you of all people would be just as competent as Amon."

"Not if the way she took on when I came here and started rawhiding her," the small Texan corrected, showing no sign of having heard the flattering reference to himself. "You told me neither she, her husband, or brother mixed with folks around town, Counselor. Could be, if she'd only heard about it and thought I'd never worn a badge before, she figured you'd just taken me on as a fast gun to keep things running smooth until Amon was back on his feet. She sure didn't act like she reckoned I was long on brains, or know-how, so she'd conclude there wasn't a thing to worry about with me handling things."

"That could be it," Sutherland conceded.

"The thing is," Clitheroe said quietly, and gestured to the books he had examined. "What do we do about the things I've discovered in these? There's a sizable sum of money missing and, being one of the depositors, I'd like to know where I stand."

"So would I," Sutherland admitted frankly. "We'll have to report what's happened to the appropriate authorities in Prescott, and I'll issue a court order to hold everything that's left under escrow until a judgment has been reached."

"That's going to be inconvenient for a lot of us," the storekeeper remarked in a pensive fashion.

"I don't doubt it," the attorney answered. "But it would have been more than just inconvenient if they'd got away with things as they intended."

"Was I you, Counselor," Dusty drawled, exuding the deference of one making a suggestion to a much senior and more experienced person, "I'd get everything that's left put under lock and put a marked seal over the lock."

"Will you help me attend to it?" Sutherland requested.

"I'd like to leave it to you and Mr. Clitheroe, sir," Dusty requested. "There're a couple of questions I want to ask her brother down to the jailhouse."

★ ★ ★

Thrusting herself from where she had been crouching over Winnie Ashwell, Calamity Jane swung a right cross many a man would have liked to be able to duplicate; it caught Doxie Rimmer on the cheek and staggered her sideways. While this removed the immediate threat posed by the buxom little rusty-brunette, it left the redhead exposed to Fifi le Planchet. However, bearing in mind the footwear of the willowy grizzled-brunette, she anticipated how the intended attack was to be launched. Sure enough, Fifi hauled up the thin skirt with both hands and her left leg rose with a ballet dancer's grace.

Although the kick was swift, Calamity decided that the grizzled-brunette lacked the skill of someone well-trained in *savate;* she had fought a girl practiced in the French system of fist and foot fighting while visiting New

Orleans.[1] Furthermore, she had learned a thing or two about the fighting method from Belle "the Rebel Spy" Boyd, who was exceptionally proficient at all aspects of it.[2] Cupping and throwing up her hands, she caught the rising ankle in them. Then, giving a surging and twisting heave, she caused her would-be assailant to turn an involuntary half-somersault.

Even as Fifi was released, coming down on her back with a thud, the redhead guessed that her predicament was not at an end. Sitting up and gasping breathless profanities, the Junoesque dyed-blonde named Winnie grabbed Calamity by the left ankle and tried to sink teeth into her thigh. Although the sturdy material of Calamity's Levi's pants prevented serious injury, the bite was still painful, and the tug on her limb caused her to topple forward. Breaking her fall with her hands as she would have done after an unexpected fall from a horse, the redhead sent her free foot backward. Caught in the face by the sole, Winnie might have been grateful that she was struck with a moccasin and not a boot. Regardless, she released her hold and rocked back with blood trickling from her nostrils.

Although having liberated herself from the grasping hands, Calamity knew that she was

1. Told in THE BULLWHIP BREED.
2. Meetings Calamity Jane had with Belle "the Rebel Spy" Boyd are recorded in THE BAD BUNCH *and* THE WHIP AND THE WAR LANCE. *Information about the career of Belle Boyd can be found in various volumes of the Civil War and Floating Outfit series.*

far from being out of danger. The three women so far not involved in the melee began to move forward in a menacing fashion, showing that they meant to come to their friend's aid.

At that moment Steffie Willis, having passed unnoticed through the woodland guided by the voices coming from the clearing, let her presence become known. She had been raised with five brothers and knew few other playmates until she moved to a town in her early teens, so she had grown up as a tomboy and gained a proficiency at physical conflict. Nor had she forgotten what she was taught since there had been times as a nurse when she needed to use methods harsher than mere words to subdue a drunken or otherwise obstreperous patient.

Rushing to meet the quartet, the buxom ash-blonde started throwing punches with such efficiency that a shapely rusty-brunette and a comely black-haired woman almost matching Winnie in height and physical attributes were sent sprawling backward. However, her hair was grabbed by the third member of the group she had tackled, a girl with auburn hair and dimensions similar to her own, who started to pull with a vigor that destroyed Steffie's bun and hurt enough to make her instinctively retaliate in the same fashion. Giving vent to squeals of rage and suffering, the two women spun in a circle away from the others. Not unexpectedly, they were not permitted to settle their differences on a one-to-one basis.

As Calamity and her assailants were coming to their feet, the two with whom Steffie first made contact were returning to the fray. From that moment, as the redhead would declare with pride and not a little enjoyment when recounting the event in later years, one hell of a fight took place in the clearing.

The methods employed by the combatants ranged from skilled use of fists and feet, mostly by the redhead and the ash-blonde, to variations on the theme of hair-pulling and other female tactics. Soon they all were showing bruising, and some had blood flowing from the nose or mouth. In one respect, however, they all might have considered themselves fortunate. Because of the strictures laid down by Derek Hatton and Steven Scott before sending the women to take revenge on Calamity, the type of womanly fighting that can cause a disfiguring injury could not be put to effective use. The gloves worn by the six women prevented them from using their nails for scratching, and even in the heat of the conflict, none thought of baring their hands so they could do so. Nor, as their respective ways of life and personal inclinations were not conducive to the luxury of growing long nails, were Calamity and Steffie any better able to do so. Not that they bothered trying; instead they devoted their attention to methods they considered likely to lead to delivering a coup de grâce.

Although their antagonists were at no point able to continue fighting as a complete group— one or another having been briefly incapacitated at every point in the fracas—neither Calamity nor Steffie found an opportunity to render any one of them down permanently *hors de combat*. At one point, finding herself engaged solely against Winnie and having attained a position where she appeared to have a chance to tear some of the now tangled and sweat-matted dyed-blonde hair out by its black roots, the redhead received a kick in the center of the back from Fifi that caused her to let go. Tackled by the slender grizzled-brunette, Calamity and Fifi went down and two other saloon workers dived forward to produce a mound of furiously struggling femininity. Later, using her superior fistic skills, Steffie was giving the black-haired and auburn-haired women cause to regret having agreed to accompany Winnie. But before she could deliver a knockout blow to either, Doxie grabbed her by the hair from behind, and she was compelled by the pain of the pulling to turn her energies in that direction.

Both the redhead and the ash-blonde were in better physical condition than any of the other women, whose way of life was not conducive to a high level of fitness, so except when they came into close proximity, neither had to pay particular attention to whom she was attacking. Nor, in their eagerness to repay the suffering inflicted upon them, did the attackers pay as much attention to the matter as they should have. This was particularly advantageous for their opponents when groups of combatants found themselves in a mindless scrum where the intention was to maul at the nearest human flesh not one's own.

When this happened, the saloon workers were likely to inflict suffering on an associate rather than their intended victims. In fact, for a short time Doxie and the black-haired woman appeared to be settling a private disagreement. They went rolling away from the others and continued fighting each other with vigor until Winnie dragged them apart by the hair and flung them toward Calamity and Steffie, then followed to add her weight to the attack.

Although neither Calamity nor Steffie realized it, they too inflicted unintentional punishment on one another. Finding her gasping mouth in proximity with a plump and shapely leg, Calamity bit its calf, causing pain without breaking the skin, and prompting Steffie to moan in agony. Likewise, a bang from the ash-blonde's badly directed elbow resulted in the discoloring and swelling of the redhead's left eye.

Clothing was just as unintentionally wrenched at, and was frequently torn away by wildly clutching hands. The sturdy Levi's worn by Calamity were the least susceptible to such mistreatment. Nevertheless, her shirt was ripped off, and she had to wriggle free from her woolen undershirt to liberate her arms when it was drawn up. At any other time, Steffie would have been embarrassed by having the bodice of her gingham dress damaged until it fell to dangle around her hips and the loss of the undergarment below left her bare to the waist. However, in the heat of the conflict, she hardly knew that her well-developed, jutting bosom had been exposed.

Before long, everybody else was reduced to a similar condition. Fifi was left in only short-legged pantalets. Doxie, having come from the cantina clad only in a dress, gloves, and slippers, was reduced to an *au naturel* state, but she paid not the slightest attention to her nudity.

The pace of the unremitting struggle began to take its toll. The combatants found it increasingly harder to replenish their lungs with air, the uncovered portions of their bodies glistened as skin was soaked by copiously flowing perspiration, and their much-abused hair turned into tangled and sweat-sodden messes. Blows and slaps were beginning to resemble tired pushes, and there was none of the former speed with which the saloon girls returned to the fray when separated from it. Fortunately, because of their better physical condition, Calamity and Steffie felt the ill effects later than their assailants did. In addition, each woman possessed a nature that refused to allow her to give in regardless of her exhaustion and suffering. The realization of what their fate would be if they suffered defeat gave them an added inducement.

Doxie succumbed first. At the bottom of a mound of weakly struggling women, her buxom body was squashed against the ground. This proved more than she could endure, and she lapsed into unconsciousness. When the others rolled away and separated to crawl tiredly to their feet, she lay spread-eagled on the grass and the only movement from her was the rise and fall of her bosom.

Having knocked Winnie away with a round-house punch from her right fist, Calamity turned to meet Fifi's wobbly-legged approach. Showing a bad appraisal of her own condition, the grizzled-brunette attempted another kick, but it never got higher than horizontal. Once again her ankle was caught by the redhead's hands. This time, however, the swing it received turned her in a half-circle. As she came around, she took a right cross to the jaw that sent her sprawling supine across the reddish-brunette younger woman, and after a brief writhing of her willowy body she went limp.

Going to where Steffie was trading exhausted slaps with the auburn- and black-haired women, the redhead grabbed the latter by the left wrist. She saw the ash-blonde obtain a similar hold on the auburn-haired woman, and she remembered how she had helped end another fight in which she and a friend had become embroiled.[3] Fortunately, Steffie was not so exhausted as to be unable to act upon the instructions that were gasped out. Bracing themselves and calling upon what little remained of their flagging energy, the friends started to swing their captives around at arm's length. Then they had a piece of unexpected luck. Staggering forward on legs that looked hardly able to bear her weight, Winnie came between the two women being swung by their wrists.

Letting out breathless wails as they realized what was coming, but too fatigued to avoid it, the two women were crashed against their leader. After the collision, they peeled away from Winnie like the skin of a banana to alight with arms and legs splayed and looks of utter stupefaction on their faces.

Although Winnie remained standing, her arms dangled limply downward. The glazed expres-

3. Told in TROUBLE TRAIL.

sion in her right eye and the discoloration and puffiness of the left made her look as though she was what a professional pugilist would have referred to as "out on her feet." However, she was not allowed to collapse of her own accord, which would have happened shortly. Unwilling to take any chances, Calamity and Steffie forced themselves to make what each fervently hoped would be a final blow and sent simultaneous punches to opposite sides of the dyed-blonde's jaw. Each woman knew there was no danger of Winnie being able to rise for some time when she pitched backward and descended flaccidly atop Fifi and Doxie's recumbent bodies.

Gasping in air and bracing themselves with hands on their thighs, the sweat-sodden and half-clad redhead and the even more disheveled ash-blonde looked around warily. Each had a blackened eye, a bloody nose, and a mottling of bruises, but all of their assailants bore at least as much damage. Calamity had lost her moccasins some time earlier, but her Levi's had withstood everything. For her part, Steffie retained her dress—although it was now torn from the hem to the level of her upper thigh—her ruined bodice was still trailing, though her shoes were gone, and her surviving stocking trailed about her left foot like a rumpled ankle sock.

"Do you feel as bad as you look?" the redhead gasped after surveying her companion wryly for a moment.

"*Worse*, I'd say," the ash-blonde replied in a similar breathless fashion.

"There's a stream in the woods back of the

clearing, I recollect," Calamity said, having looked around the area hunting for some fresh meat. "We'd best go 'n' freshen up, then figure some way to get dressed enough to go to my wagon, where I've got some duds we can use."

"All right," Steffie replied, then turned her gaze to the still-unmoving bodies of their defeated attackers. "Damn it, I know now how Doc Leroy must feel."

"How come?" the redhead inquired, knowing the man named to have been a regular member of the Wedge trail crew and possessed of considerable medical ability even though he had never qualified as a doctor.

"He was always complaining that every time he shot somebody and didn't kill him, he wound up having to 'tend to the wound," the ash-blonde explained. "And now I've got to make sure none of them are badly hurt before we leave them."

4

IT DIDN'T GET *THAT* FAR

"Am I *pleased* you've come back, Dusty," Rusty Willis said as the small Texan entered the office at the jailhouse. Of just over medium height, with a stocky and powerful build, Rusty had hair that indicated how his sobriquet had been acquired and a ruggedly good-looking face that would normally be cheerful but now looked grim. His attire was that of a Texas cowhand, but he wore the badge of a deputy sheriff and had served as a peace

38

officer in addition to being a regular member of the Wedge from the days when they took trail herds from Texas to Kansas.[1] He carried a walnut-handled Colt Artillery Model Peacemaker in a well-designed holster on his right thigh, and while he did not claim to be fast with it, he was competent enough for his needs. "There's a real *bad* feeling going around town."

"Aye, that there is," Angus McTavish agreed from where he stood by the right-side window before Dusty could speak. Tall, gaunt, with a face that seemed to be bearing all the sorrows of the world, he was wearing his usual garb, the most noticeable item of which was a knitted woolen bonnet with a pompom on top and trews in the tartan of his clan; a Colt Storekeeper Model Peacemaker was tucked into his waistband. What happened the only time somebody had tried to make fun of them was part of Child City's mythology. "Which is why I closed down—and it's a muckle amount of trade I'll be losing."

"There's some around who wouldn't want a *mucky* amount of trade," Dusty asserted. He knew the meaning of the the actual word and was aware that the tall, lean, and dourly craggy-faced Scottish owner of the Arizona State Saloon was no more parsimonious than Counselor Edward Sutherland pretended to be. His Texas drawl became serious before the correction to his pronunciation could be made. "What's up?"

1. When and where Rusty Willis served as a peace officer is told in QUIET TOWN.

"There started to be a whole lot of talk about how it wasn't right that brother of Mrs. Harman's was just sitting in jail instead of getting what she and her husband did for killing young Canoga and dropping him into that unused well the way he was," the saloonkeeper explained as Rusty glanced his way. "But that's not surprising. Toby was always a popular young feller, and having just become a father makes it worse. Anyway, as soon as I saw the way things were going, I told my bartenders to put the corks back in the bottles and close the doors."

"*Gracias,* Angus," the small Texan said. "Was anybody yelling out for something to be done to put things right?"

"It didn't get *that* far," McTavish admitted. "Just started to be more'n talk about how it didn't seem right, but I figured closing up the bar might be an easy way of stopping it. I once before saw what happened for something similar and knew it would only be a matter of time before somebody came up with that notion."

"Weren't there any objections to you doing it?" Dusty asked. He had had one experience of how quickly sentiments could be aroused to a pitch where a lynching was decided upon by otherwise honest and law-abiding citizens.

"A few, but I said I'd forgotten it was Flora McDonald's birthday and no self-respecting Scot is expected to do business on it," McTavish replied. "There was some mutters, but my boys had their bung-starters and the girls began easing the customers out by saying they were pleased to be given the day off—with *pay,* as that was a tradition on the day. Blast it, they've been working for me so long they're starting to *think* like Scots."

"They do say as you reap, so shall you sow," the small Texan pointed out, but he was genuinely grateful for the forethought shown by McTavish and serious under his veneer of levity, as was the saloonkeeper.

"Aye," McTavish agreed. "Although I believe you'll find the exact quotation is 'As *ye* reap, so shall *ye* sow.' "

"Not in Texas," Rusty claimed. He also had a need to relieve the feeling of tension. "Anyways, I've got Thorny in back nursing a scatter in case anybody figures on sneaking in that way."

"Smart figuring," Dusty praised, knowing he could count on his fellow Texan to take such a wise precaution without waiting for orders. "But with the Arizona State closed for Flora McDonald's birthday, they shouldn't be able to get enough liquor down them to start thinking all noble and brave about getting evens for Toby."

"Unless that bunch at the cantina start letting them have it," McTavish reminded. "I know they don't have everything set up ready for opening yet, but a bar and somebody to draw the corks is all that's needed to sell liquor."

"You want for me to go take a look?" Rusty inquired. He had failed to take into account that there was now another source in Child City from which hard liquor could be obtained. This information had been uncovered in the examination of the account books at the Cattlemen's Bank by Amos Clitheroe.

"Nope," the small Texan replied. "Should there be trouble you'll be needed here, and seeing you out and about might prod somebody into starting it." Then, puzzled upon realizing that the third of his deputies was neither in the office nor otherwise accounted for, he went on, "Where-at's Calam?"

"Went to 'tend to her team down to the wagons," Rusty replied with a grin. "You know her, she doesn't even trust Tumac and the rest of Dobe's boys to do that. Could be she's finished by now, but heard what's doing 'n' concluded to stay 'round 'n' about keeping an eye on the way things're going."

"That'd be like her," Dusty admitted with a grin. He knew the girl and admired her for her rugged spirit of independence, even though there had been times when he wished she had kept it under control. "Just so long as she doesn't try to take on whatever she meets up with on her lonesome, which would be just as like her as well. That gal can sure find fuss. There's no wonder folks call her Calamity."

If the girl had been able to hear Dusty speak of her habit of finding trouble at that moment, she would have been inclined to agree with it for once. She was in the closing stages of the roughest fight of her life.

Before any more was said, a man came into the office.

"This message has just come in, Captain Fog," the man stated, holding out a folded buff-colored sheet of paper, which all three occupants of the office had no trouble recognizing.

Tall, slim, bespectacled, and passably good-looking, albeit with a pallor that gave support

42

to the reason he had given for coming west, as usual William Morris was dressed and spoke more like a moderately well-off clerk in a major business back east than might be expected of the agent at the Wells Fargo depot in Child City. That he had never been seen to carry a gun did not arouse any comment, since the need for him to be armed had never arisen. He claimed to have an illness he was trying to have cured by the local climate, so although he was a skillful telegraphist and general organizer, he had his manual duties performed by three men he had brought with him to serve as his staff. His predecessor had been sent into retirement on account of his age by the company's head supervisor for Arizona Territory at Prescott.

Being single, as was his predecessor, Morris had continued to allow the domestic duties usually performed by a married agent's family—such as accommodating passengers overnight or while awaiting other means of continuing a journey—to remain in the hands of the Summers Hotel's owners, and they were grateful this added source of revenue was not to be curtailed. Otherwise, he discharged his duties in a satisfactory manner, as did the hard-looking trio of men he had brought with him, and no complaints had been made about any of them. Although Dusty had seen Morris around town on a few occasions, they had not become acquainted, because he took little part in social activities and never went into the Arizona State Saloon—because, he said, of the orders he had received from the doctor who sent him west. For all his frequent references to his ailment, he never sought the services of the local physician or explained why.

" 'Dusty,' " the small Texan read, having opened the standard telegraph message form used by Wells Fargo. " 'Pleased you sent nursemaids. Ranches already have owners. Staying on for a while. Do you want nursemaids back? Stone.' "

"I hope the word 'nursemaids' isn't an error on the part of the Prescott depot, Captain Fog," Morris said in his usual pedantic fashion and New England accent. "It doesn't seem quite right to me."

"It's cowhand humor, and that doesn't often seem right to anybody else," Dusty explained, but he had read what was intended by the sender and did not care for the connotations. He concluded that Stone Hart and Major Wilson Eardle had run into some kind of dangerous situation either during the journey or since reaching the capital city, and that there had been an unanticipated development on paying the visit to the territorial land agent. The first conclusion prompted his next words: "Do you get a lot of errors from Prescott?"

"Not more than from anywhere else," the agent replied a trifle stiffly. "But *some* operators occasionally do make an error—although it is mostly due to the handwriting of the sender."

"Uh-huh!" the small Texan grunted, a non-committal sound he often found useful when no other comment seemed called for. He was amused by the way Morris had come to the defense of the other telegraph operators. Then, thinking of the first part of the message from the boss of the Wedge ranch, he asked in a seemingly offhand manner, "Do you get a lot of messages for or from folk in Prescott?"

"Some," the agent said vaguely and in a seemingly uninterested fashion. "But many others have to be routed through our telegraph office there."

"Would you have had any sent to folks in Prescott over the last three days?" the small Texan inquired.

"A few," Morris admitted.

"Do you keep any record of them?"

"Of course. It's company policy to do so, as it allows a check to be kept on the contents in case of complaints."

"Could I look over your records, was I so minded?"

"Well, it isn't company policy to break confidentiality with our clients," Morris said in slightly pompous tone, as though he was dealing with an impertinent suggestion and an infringement upon his authority.

"Jim Hume's always told me Wells Fargo's agents are expected to cooperate with the law on *everything* that comes up," Dusty countered.

"You know Mr. Hume?" Morris queried, aware that the man in question was the company's very competent chief detective.

"We worked alongside one another while I was running the law in Mulrooney, Kansas," the small Texan replied. "For a Yankee out of New York's Catskill Mountains, he's surely a cigar-loving hell-twister comes trouble, and a real good man to have along when the river's rising so the water's coming up over the willows. I could telegraph and ask him to say whether you should help me should I need it."[2]

"That won't be necessary," the agent stated. He had heard enough about James B. Hume to have no doubt that the permission would be forthcoming. He was also aware that there was far more to the man he was addressing than appeared on the surface, although this was the first time they had been in a conversation, or even in close proximity. "You may come and check on the register anytime you wish, Sheriff."

"*Gracias,* Mr. Morris," Dusty drawled, "I'll likely drop by later to do it."

"May I ask why?" the agent queried.

"No particular reason, I'll admit," the small Texan lied, with the appearance of veracity. "It's just something my pappy used to tell me could prove useful when he was teaching me to be a peace officer back to Rio Hondo County. Can be handy to know if anybody 'specially important's being asked to come visiting so everything can be got ready for them when they arrive."

"There's been nothing of that nature as far as I can recollect," Morris claimed, then gave a shrug. "But feel free to come and look for yourself whenever you wish."

"I'll do that," Dusty drawled, his manner

2. We have not been informed what was entailed in the cooperation between Dusty Fog and James B. Hume at Mulrooney, Kansas.

implying that he felt nothing more need be said on the matter. "Thanks for fetching this along yourself."

"I had to," the agent stated in a manner that suggested he considered such a menial task beneath his dignity. "My men were all busy, and all of the boys I can usually send when messages come in are hanging around that old cantina."

"That figures," Dusty said under his breath, but he sensed that Rusty and McTavish shared the sentiment.

"Looks like they went *there*," the stocky Texan commented after Morris had left the office. "Seeing as those two jaspers who're running it don't celebrate Flora McDonald's birthday by closing up."

"That's the way it looks," the small Texan agreed. "I hope that Calam has gone down there keeping an eye on things so as she can get back to let us know if things are going bad."

★ ★ ★

"All right, you sorry-looking bunch. We whupped you fair 'n' square and could likely do it ag'in, only we're not fixing to do it right now!"

Calamity Jane was making ready to cope with the distaff side of the cantina's employees.

At the stream, the redhead and Steffie Willis had contrived to remove the superficial effects of the fight they had had with the six saloon girls. Having stripped and bathed in the clear water, they had dried themselves as best they could and donned the remnants of their clothing

47

again. Then, showing a knowledge of primitive kinds of medication, they had used the syrupy gum obtained from the blisterlike swellings on the trunk of a balsam fir tree to stop the blood that still trickled from their nostrils and minor abrasions. Feeling better—although the ash-blonde said she wished she knew who had bitten her calf, which still stung—they walked slowly and somewhat stiffly back to the clearing. There they saw that the women were all sitting up or showing other signs of recovery. Although none were yet making any attempt to get to their feet, Calamity was glad she had taken the precaution of buckling on her gunbelt before she and Steffie returned.

"Wh—What are you going to do with us?" Fifi le Planchet asked, eyeing the bullwhip on the redhead's belt with some apprehension. She remembered having heard how well its owner could use it.

"Nothing, so long as I don't need to," Calamity answered, keeping her right hand on the handle of the whip. She noticed that Fifi's alarm was clearly shared by the other five women. "I'm going to get some duds for me 'n' Steffie to use to get back to town without folks seeing us the way we are now. Not that I figure the menfolks'd mind the chance."

"How about *us*?" Doxie Rimmer wailed. Calamity's reference to clothes had caused her to become aware of her own semiclad condition again.

"You get back any way you can," Calamity answered in an indifferent tone. "Only, afore you start at it, don't ask me *why*, but Steffie wants to look you over 'n' make sure none of

48

you is bad hurt. She's a trained nurse 'n' can do it if none of you wants to take up what you started and we finished."

Walking forward and meeting no opposition, the ash-blonde set about the examination of her former antagonists. The story of how she had delivered the baby born to Matilda Canoga had reached them, and they felt grateful to her for showing them consideration as well. Much to her relief, she discovered that although every one of the women had suffered more surface damage than was inflicted upon herself and Calamity, none showed signs of having sustained internal injury.

The task completed, Steffie found that the redhead had contrived to offset the damage to her tartan shirt in such a way that it covered her bare bosom. In addition, Calamity had gathered the means to fix the torn skirt of the gingham dress in a way that would suffice to let them reach her freight wagon and obtain more adequate attire.

What neither Calamity nor Steffie took into account was that the vehicle was on the opposite side of town and, unless they went around the outskirts, reaching it would entail crossing the main street.

5
BUSHWHACK *RIGHT,* MARK!

Unaware of the problems besetting Calamity Jane and Dusty Fog in Child City—although, knowing her as he did, he would not have been oversurprised to find out how she had

49

become embroiled in the fight—Mark Counter was taking advantage of the fact that everything was running smoothly at the first bunch ground he had selected. Remembering that Dusty Fog had treated him in the same fashion when they found themselves acting respectively as roundup captain and straw boss, as the second in command was known, he had decided to let his replacement in the latter capacity learn at first hand what was entailed by the position in the work upon which they were engaged.[1] Doing so would allow him to escape the multifarious duties that were going to be his lot for a short while by going out as if he were just one of the hands to help search for and gather cattle.

Because Mark's own seventeen-hand bloodbay stallion was better suited to traveling long distances at a good speed than to working cattle, although he had used it for that purpose on occasion, he was using a *bayos azafranados* gelding selected from the Wedge's remuda. Saffron-hued, between dun and sorrel, it was not quite as hefty as his private horse. However, since he was a light rider capable of taking less out of his mount than a lighter but less skilled person, it was up to carrying his weight, and that had been an important factor in his selection.

Regardless of where he was or what was going on around him, Mark tended to stand out in any company. On first seeing him, the

---

1. When Dusty Fog and Mark Counter served respectively as roundup captain and straw boss is recorded in THE MAN FROM TEXAS.

beautiful and talented woman who became Dusty's wife had said Mark looked like the Greek god Apollo with the physique of Hercules. His six-foot-three-inch frame was topped by golden-blond hair and a tanned, almost classically handsome face with intelligence in its strong lines. There was a great width to his shoulders. Below, his torso slimmed to a narrow waist before opening out to proportionately sized hips set on long and powerful legs clearly as well-muscled as the biceps that showed beneath the ample sleeves of his shirt. Large and clearly possessed of exceptional strength, he nevertheless gave the impression of being quick and agile. In fact, as had often been proved in the past, he could move with commendable rapidity when called for in any situation.[2]

Although purely functional and evidently worn for the work he was doing, the blond giant's attire looked in some respects like that of a dandy. There was a black leather band decorated by silver conchas on his white Texas-style J. B. Stetson hat. The rest of his attire had clearly been made to his measure; such an excellent fit could not have been achieved from the ready-to-wear shelves of a store, even one in a major city. Made by a master craftsman, his brown leather *buscadero* gunbelt carried two ivory-handled Colt Cavalry Model Peacemaker revolvers in its contoured holsters. These, too, were by no means decorative. Despite their seven-and-a-half-inch barrels he had acquired a skill that was acknowledged as being second only

2. Details of Mark Counter's family background and special qualifications are given in Appendix Two.

to that of his small dusty-blond *amigo*, the Rio Hondo gun wizard, Dusty Fog, in speed of withdrawal and shooting accuracy.

Unlike Dusty in Child City—or the Ysabel Kid at Prescott, for that matter—Mark had experienced only a few minor problems since circumstances had compelled him to take over as roundup captain and relinquish the less demanding duties of straw boss. These were still open-range days—with stock allowed to roam at will until needed—and the crew he had under his control had come from the four ranches that formed Spanish Grant County. The foremen of the two properties currently without owners had been instructed to participate by Counselor Edward Sutherland in his capacity as justice of the peace for the area. The ruling was based on the grounds that to do so would prove beneficial for whoever eventually owned the ranches and save them the expense of a similar gather of their own stock after taking over.

The crews of the spreads had always been on good terms—even Ed Leshin of the Vertical Triple E had been unaware of the machinations carried out by Eustace Edgar Eisteddfod with the intention of stirring up trouble between Stone Hart and Major Wilson Eardle—and the men assigned from each for the roundup were working together amicably. As was to be expected—honest cowhands being the kind of men they were—there was some rivalry between the members of the different outfits, but this was conducted on an amiable basis and was beneficial, since it ensured that everybody did his best for the honor of the brand he served. There had not been a single protest over the venting of the CM brand on the cattle that had belonged to Cornelius MacLaine, to be replaced by Stone Hart's Wedge insignia. In fact, all the hands from the other ranches had volunteered to give assistance.

Dusty had been called to Child City to temporarily assume the duties of county sheriff, and this had necessitated a change in the management of the roundup. The blond giant was asked to take over the position vacated by Dusty, and so another second in command was needed. The selection of Jimmy Conlin, the foreman of Eardle's AW, had been carried out through the drawing of straws in the presence of witnesses and was accepted as a satisfactory arrangement by all concerned. Mark had already acquired enough faith in Conlin's ability to have had no qualms over leaving him in charge at the bunch ground while he himself sought a brief period of relaxation before tackling the multitude of details and problems that are faced by a trail boss.

Holding the well-trained gelding to a steady walk as he proceeded along the open bottom of a valley with a fair number of bushes and small trees on each of its gently rising slopes, Mark was having no difficulty hazing along the small bunch of cattle he and his companion had already collected. These were to be taken to the bunch ground for identification of ownership and for changing the brands from CM to Wedge and from Lazy Scissors to AW where necessary. The status of any unmarked animals, many sure to be calves or yearlings that had separated from their mothers—and therefore failing to provide the long-accepted source of establishing right to possession—would also need to be determined.

Should ownership be impossible to ascertain, by agreement between Stone Hart, Major Eardle, and Counselor Sutherland speaking on behalf of the two ranches left without proprietors, the mavericks in question would be divided equally between the four spreads. Nor did the problems with the gathered animals end there. Because of the inborn proclivities of the semidomesticated longhorn cattle to roam vast distances, there would almost certainly be some belonging to spreads outside Spanish Grant County—in which case, the owners would need to be notified by telegraph and arrangements made for collection or some other means of disposal.

Such matters were only a few of the duties required of a roundup captain.

Known only as Dude, the man chosen as the blond giant's companion had for some time been acquainted with Dusty and the other members of the floating outfit formed at the instigation of General Jackson Baines "Ole Devil" Hardin for the OD Connected ranch in Rio Hondo County, Texas.[3] He had always tended to be a drifter, and although often asked, never took steady employment for any length of time. However, having come on the trail drive by which Stone Hart brought a herd of cattle to Spanish Grant County—although he had

3. Two occasions when Dude was in contact with members of General Ole Devil Hardin's floating outfit are recorded in TRAIL BOSS *and* GUNS IN THE NIGHT.

not previously been a member of the crew—
he had taken a liking to the way things were
run and, deciding the time had come for a
change in his ways, accepted the offer to stay
on at the Wedge ranch.

Good-looking, almost as tall and well-built
as Mark, Dude also wore work-stained clothes
of the somewhat dandified style, a habit that
had given rise to his sobriquet. Nevertheless,
to eyes that knew the signs he had the appearance
of being a tophand, and indeed he was competent
in all aspects of the work he was called upon
to carry out. The Peacemakers in the holsters
of his well-designed gunbelt had ivory handles
but were of the shorter-barreled Artillery
Model. While he could not claim the speed that
Dusty Fog and the blond giant were capable
of, and would never have claimed to be a
gunfighter, he had occasionally been compelled
to prove himself adequate in matters *pistolero*
to ensure his survival.

Having gone off in search of any cattle that
might be in the vicinity, Dude was returning
to report that there were none to be found.
Topping a ridge brought him into view of
Mark and the animals already collected, moving some distance away along the valley below.
As he was about to go down the slope, a flock
of Gambel's quail erupted from the bushes nearby. He idly watched the dainty birds, with their
teardrop feather topknots erect, speed away
in the manner that made them much sought
after as game birds by aficionados of the
rapidly developing sport of wing-shooting in
those regions of California and Arizona where
the species was to be found. Although he

could not be included in that number, he enjoyed their succulent taste when prepared by the cook for the Wedge, Chow Willicka, and he wished he had a shotgun with him now. However, he was aware that much work was to be done, and he had not burdened his red-roan gelding with even his Winchester Model of 1873 rifle.

Silently cursing his luck, the cowhand saw the birds suddenly swing away from the clump of bushes toward which they had been flying. Through the bushes he noticed a splash of color not in keeping with its surrounding, since no foliage he had ever seen was of a dark blue hue. Looking closer, he discerned movement and enough partially concealed, but obviously human, shapes to realize that there was something of sinister intent being planned by whoever had caused the quail to change directions.

The supposition was correct.

Having been given instructions to go out and disrupt the work on the roundup, Jack Dromey and Steven Burak had been making their way across the rolling range country toward a spot they believed the first bunch ground would be situated. Although their attire might have led anybody new to the West to assume that they were cowhands, more experienced eyes would have detected enough evidence to know that this assumption was not correct. Regardless of their clothing, they had all the earmarks of hired guns.

Studying cautiously the slope they were ascending, they had seen Mark moving the cattle along the bottom of the valley in their direction. Since they had just recently come south from Wyoming, neither recognized him. Still, after studying his clothing and armament, they concluded that—in addition to serving the purpose for which they had been hired—he would be worth shooting for the loot he had on his person. Leaving their horses tied to saplings beyond the edge of the rim, they had taken Winchester rifles from their saddle boots, cocked each action, and charged the chambers with bullets from the tubular magazines. Then they had advanced without being detected until finding a place offering concealment some fifty yards from where he would have to go by.

Satisfied that they could do so without being detected by their intended victim, Dromey and Burak began to raise the rifles to their shoulders.

Just as the pair of hired guns were aligning their sights, Dude made his presence known in no uncertain fashion.

"Bushwhack *right,* Mark!" the cowhand bellowed at the top of his voice.

Having delivered what he considered to be a comprehensive warning, although prudence would have suggested he show more caution, Dude drew and cocked his right-hand Colt while setting the red-roan moving forward at a rapid gait. He had no idea who the men in the bushes might be, but he had no doubt they were up to no good. With a friend in danger, that was all he needed to know. However, before he had gone many feet, he sensed that his warning had come too late.

"Take the big 'n'!" Burak snarled when he

heard the warning. He started to swing around with the butt of the rifle cradled against the shoulder of the dark-blue shirt that, along with the behavior of the Gambel's quail, had betrayed his and his companion's presence in the bushes. "I'll fix the other bastard's wagon!"

Without responding verbally, Dromey completed sighting his Winchester and squeezed the trigger. Through the swirl of white smoke from the powder that left the muzzle, he saw the white Stetson jerk away and the blond giant pitch over the left side of the horse to alight on the ground. Startled by the sudden departure of its rider, the gelding went forward a few hurried strides; then its training to remain still when its open-ended reins were allowed to dangle free brought it to a stop.

"I got the big son of a bitch!" exclaimed Dromey, the shorter, more thickset, and younger of the pair.

There was no reply from Burak, who was concentrating on what he was preparing to do. Sighting on the approaching rider, whose horse was being urged to move faster, Burak squeezed off a shot. Crouching forward to offer a smaller target, Dude heard the .44-caliber flat-nosed bullet strike his gelding in the neck. A scream burst from it and, its neck broken, it started to go down. The cowhand's excellent ability as a rider was all that saved him. Jerking his sharp-toed and high-heeled boots from the stirrup irons, he threw himself aside as the stricken animal collapsed beneath him.

Using the skill he had acquired during a lifetime spent—for some period of each day, at least—on the back of a horse, Dude contrived to alight on his feet without losing his grip on the butt of his Colt. However, appreciating the danger he was still in, he did not attempt to remain erect and use his revolver. Instead, after being narrowly missed by another bullet, he made a plunging bound that carried him behind the nearest bush. He wondered how Mark was faring, but, certain he was still being covered by the rifle that had killed his horse, he did not try to satisfy his curiosity. Instead, he began to advance from cover to cover in the hope of attaining a distance from which he could employ the Colt to greater effect than would have been possible where he alighted.

Satisfied that his bullet had flown as it was intended, Dromey lowered the rifle until it was at arm's length before him and darted from the bushes. He was determined to reach and help himself to the blond giant's belongings while Burak was occupied in dealing with the second cowhand. However, as he was leaving the shelter of the bushes, he discovered he had made a terrible mistake.

Dude's warning had been uttered just in time. A quick glance to his right had told Mark all he needed to know. Putting to use his superb coordination and capability for rapid movement, he was thrusting himself to the left when a shot was fired his way. Judging by the way in which the Stetson was ripped from his head, the lead passing through the top of its crown without touching his skull, he knew he had had a very narrow escape.

Like every cowhand, the blond giant had acquired expertise in all facets of riding. Despite his size and bulk, this riding skill allowed him to go down without feeling more than a jolt and alight on the springy grass of the valley's bottom. Going down, he brought the right-side Colt from its holster and twisted onto his side so the weapon was concealed by his body. When he saw the hired gun coming from the bushes, he lay still to give the impression that he had been hit. He was aware that the distance separating them favored the man and rifle, so he hoped to shorten it before letting the truth of the matter become apparent. He managed to glance around without being detected after hearing the rifle shot from the bushes and the scream of Dude's stricken horse, and he was relieved to see that his companion had not been hurt. He continued to lie still.

Dromey ran from the concealment offered by the bushes and had halved the distance between himself and his supposed victim when he discovered his error. Although Mark would have preferred to allow his attacker to come closer before making his move, the blond giant concluded that he could not do so. There was another man with a rifle in the bushes whose movements needed to be accounted for, except that Dude—who was armed only with revolvers—still appeared to be holding his attention. Which meant that Mark might be called upon to help his companion, and this required that he be left free to play his part without further threat from the one who was in view.

Thrusting himself into a sitting position as swiftly as he could manage, the blond giant drew on his experiences as a gunfighter as he assessed the situation. Not only was his attacker carrying the Winchester that had come so close to sending lead into him, but the distance between them still favored the rifle over Mark's Cavalry Model Peacemaker. He concluded that there was only one solution that might serve him under the prevailing conditions, and he immediately sought to put it into effect. Locking his right elbow against his side while instinctively aligning the Colt, he squeezed the trigger and sent off the first shot. His instincts warned him that he had missed, but he was ready to cope with that contingency.

Having fired, the blond giant swiftly brought around his cupped left hand so its palm caught the spur of the hammer. With the trigger still held back, the motion caused another bullet to be discharged. Then the sequence was repeated in very rapid succession. When performed by an expert, there was no faster way to operate the single-action mechanism of the Peacemaker, which required manual cocking between shots. Because of his great strength, Mark was especially adept at this maneuver.

At each detonation, contriving to control the considerable recoil kick, the blond giant moved the barrel slightly and the bullets flew on divergent courses. The first three missed, but by a decreasing margin each time. Flying more by chance than intent, the fourth took Dromey just above his right hip. A moment later, the fifth plowed into the left side of his lower torso. Although the sixth went by harmlessly, Dromey staggered back a few steps from the double hit. However, he did not fall down, and he retained his hold on the rifle.

Letting the empty revolver drop from his hand, Mark came to his feet with a surging bound. Almost as soon as he was erect, he saw that Dromey was starting to raise the Winchester to a firing position in spite of his wounds, and he knew what must be done. Descending, he instinctively cocked the hammer of the other Colt with his left hand and brought it from its holster. He would have simply used his left hand if the range had been shorter, but he took the brief instant required to perform the so-called border shift, tossing the gun so his right fingers and thumb closed around the ivory butt. His left joined them, and he brought the revolver to shoulder level at arm's length. The method permitted more accurate shooting than would otherwise have been possible, and the blond giant put this improvement to good use.

His attacker clearly meant to carry on the fight, and despite being injured, held a weapon with a greater potential for accuracy over the distance between them. Therefore, Mark aligned the barrel of the Peacemaker in the only way that would meet the needs of the situation. When it crashed, a hole appeared in the center of Dromey's forehead and the lead burst out at the back of his skull. Although Dromey was killed instantly, a reflex action caused him to squeeze the trigger of the rifle he had been lining at Mark. However, the barrel had been sufficiently deflected for the lead to miss its intended target by a few inches, and the hired gun would never be able to make another try.

Seeing what had happened to his companion and knowing that the second cowhand was stalking him through the bushes, Burak decided that the situation had gotten dire. Swinging around, he hurried back up the slope and ran to the waiting horses. He had liberated both, mounted his own, and was riding off when Dude came into view. However, the distance between them was great enough for him to be safe from the Texan's revolvers, and he made good his escape.

6
NOBODY GETS LYNCHED
IN *MY* TOWN!

"The new law wrangler's coming fast, Dusty," Rusty Willis reported from his place by the right-side window of the sheriff's office. "Looks more'n a mite stirred up."

"Let him in when he gets here," the small Texan instructed. "Could be he's heard what's being said and is worried about his client."

About twenty minutes had gone by since William Morris, the Wells Fargo agent, had taken his departure. Without explaining his reason, Dusty Fog had asked Angus McTavish to follow Morris and have two messages dispatched by telegraph. One was to Prescott requesting that Stone Hart send back the two "nursemaids," whose help was required to care for patients unless they were urgently needed there. The second, addressed to Miss Sue Ortega care of Mrs. Maisie Simons at Backsight, requested that she inform Charles

Henry and Marvin Eldridge that there was no work available for them on a ranch in Spanish Grant County so they should gamble on finding it in some new place. The small Texan had not explained what either message meant, or why he asked that his name not be mentioned when arranging for the latter to be sent. All he had said was that he thought the owner of the Arizona State Saloon would be less likely to be the subject of hostile attentions on the street than either of his deputies should the situation they all envisaged come to pass.

Accepting the wisdom of the suggestion and refraining from trying to satisfy his curiosity as to the true meaning of the two messages, the Scot had done as requested. He had claimed he had been asked to send the second message by a cowhand passing through town the previous evening and had forgotten to do so until reaching the telegraph office with the one for Stone Hart. Using as an excuse the pretense that he wished to query the nonarrival of a shipment of liquor from a dealer, he had waited until both were passed over the wires and their contents entered in the agent's log. Then he had claimed he could not recollect the name of the man with whom he had dealt and, having no wish to get the wrong person in trouble over the omission, would have to find this out before lodging the complaint.

Leaving the Wells Fargo depot, McTavish had taken a roundabout route that led him by the old cantina. Seeing him looking over the batwing doors at the front entrance, Derek Hatton had come over to say that the closing of the Arizona State Saloon for Flora

64

McDonald's birthday had been beneficial for their business. However, the New Englander had stated misgivings over the way in which the talk among the customers was becoming increasingly hostile toward the man being held prisoner at the jailhouse. It had reached the point, Hatton asserted, where he and his partner—wanting to avoid the possibility of causing problems for Sheriff Fog—were considering shutting down before matters got any worse. Saying that might be the wisest course and promising to call back to take the offered "something on the house" later, the Scot had returned to tell Dusty all he had seen and heard.

"Who-all's out there?" Rusty called after a twist at the locked handle of the front door.

"Counselor Nigel Jones," came the reply in a voice of one who had been raised in a well-off area of New York. "I want to see the sheriff."

"Is that all right, Cap'n Fog, sir?" the Wedge cowhand inquired, sounding as if he had not already received permission for the request to be granted.

"Why, sure," the small Texan confirmed, contriving to hide his amusement over Rusty's behavior. "Let the counselor in."

If the glare directed at the Wedge cowhand was any indication, the man who entered was not amused. Around five feet seven and scrawny, he removed his black derby hat to show black hair plastered down by a liberal coating of aromatic bay rum. He had sharp and sallow features that were so parchmentlike they made him appear older than his years and were prone to show whatever he was feeling—surprising for one of his profession. However, this did not appear to have been in any way detrimental to the success of his career, if his attire was any indication. Everything he was wearing was in the latest Eastern style and of excellent cut.

"Good afternoon, Counselor," Dusty drawled, coming to his feet. "I'm sorry we had the door locked, but you may not know there could be trouble over your clients."

"I most certainly *do* know," Nigel Jones asserted, not mollified by the explanation. "I had to go see Mr. Hatton and Mr. Scott on a matter of business, and I am *very* perturbed by what was being said there."

"Would they be talking lynch rope?" Rusty inquired, having resumed his place by the window.

"Not Mr. Hatton or Mr. Scott, if that is who your deputy meant by 'they'!" the lawyer snapped, making it obvious that he regarded the rusty-haired Wedge cowhand as unworthy of a direct answer. "I realize you don't like either of them, Captain Fog, but—!"

"The only reason I've been given to feel anyways about them is that they stood back and let that mean trained fighting dog of theirs attack a *boy's* pet and got him bitten badly trying to stop them," Dusty interrupted. "Since then, I've had no cause to feel one way or the other about them. My deputy just made things sound wrong."

"Why, sure," the Wedge cowhand agreed, looking as innocent as a newborn baby. "What I meant by the 'they' was, is it any of their customers talking lynch rope. Such things generally start to happen in a drinking place, by what I've been told."

"Which same has always been my experience," the small Texan concurred. "Anyways, Counselor, you conclude that those fellers down to the cantina could have some such notions in mind?"

"I don't 'conclude' anything," Jones corrected. He was too experienced in legal technicalities to allow himself to be tricked into making a suggestion of such a nature. "I merely heard enough talk to feel concerned for the safety of my clients and came to warn you about it."

"Why, thank you 'most to death for your kindness, sir," Dusty drawled, and he could have meant the words if his tone and expression were any guide. Knowing him far better than the attorney did, Rusty was aware that this was not the case. "I can understand why you'd feel more than a mite concerned if you'd heard enough to think your clients could wind up stretching hemp without being sent to do it all right 'n' legal in front of our respected justice of the peace."

"You know it can't come to *that*, Captain Fog," Jones stated. "Apart from there being certain to be personal prejudice and bias against my clients in this town, the robbery being at the bank makes it a federal offense and must be dealt with as such, if the law is given a chance to take its course."

"It will be," the small Texan claimed, and the way in which he responded gave the impression that he was the tallest man present.

"You can bet all you own on *that*. Nobody gets lynched in *my* town."

"And, was I a religious man," Rusty put in from by the window, "I'd say amen to that. 'Cepting we could have some yahoos figuring different on it, Cap'n Fog."

"Looks like you're as right as the Injun side of a hoss, *amigo*," Dusty confirmed, having strode swiftly to the side of his temporary deputy.

Looking along the street, the small Texan assessed the potential of the group of men who were approaching. Experienced in such matters, he liked nothing of what he was deducing. A number of genuine friends and a few associates of the murder victim were present, but he tended to discount them as a significant factor. With few exceptions, they held positions of moderate standing in Child City, and the remainder were the kind of loafers who could be found on the fringes of crowds either as onlookers or active participants in any small town west of the Mississippi River. However, there were a number of others who represented a more dangerous faction.

Dusty suspected that the town being built at the point where the boundaries of the four ranches would come together—the division of the Spanish Grant had not yet taken place— had been in accordance with the Legislation of the Territory when the owner died intestate. It would—and did—serve as a neutral ground where the crews of the spreads could come together for business and social reasons. However, this had not been the only purpose served by Child City. Because of the location, it had become the gathering point for Wells Fargo stagecoach routes. Travelers headed in all directions had found it a useful point upon which to converge and take a rest from their journeys. Therefore, there was always a transient population with no permanent ties in the neighborhood, and it was from this element that Dusty expected the main trouble would come.

"How do we handle things, Captain Fog?" McTavish inquired, crossing to the rack on the wall to collect a shotgun.

"Aren't *you* getting one, Captain Fog?" Jones asked when the small Texan did not follow the other two.

"Nope," Dusty answered.

"Why not?" the lawyer queried. "I would have thought—!"

"You two stay put with the counselor and make sure *nobody* gets in—or leaves, if you know what I mean," Dusty interrupted.

"We've a pretty fair notion," Rusty asserted without so much as a glance at Jones. "Haven't we, Mr. McTavish?"

"Aye, Deputy Willis, that we have," the Scot confirmed, also with no acknowledgment of the attorney. "And you can count on us doing it, Cap'n Fog."

"*Bueno*," the small Texan drawled, then raised his voice. "Hey, Thorny, could be some fuss."

"You want me out there?" said the young Wedge cowhand, who had been selected as a deputy by the small Texan because of the cool head he had displayed in two dangerous situations.

"Nope," Dusty denied. "Keep the back door locked and, should it be tried, stop anybody coming in *any* way you have to."

"I'll do just that!" Thorny Bush promised, trying not entirely successfully to keep his excitement out of his voice.

"And watch the windows of their cells," the small Texan supplemented, hoping the youngster would continue to behave calmly and sensibly. He decided against adding a warning that whoever came should be identified as friendly or hostile before action was taken to prevent entry. "Somebody might conclude to save the cost of a trial by fixing to cut them down through them."

"Yo!" the youngster answered, using the traditional cavalry response to an order.

"Where's Calam at?" Rusty asked in a puzzled tone as he returned to the window.

"Likely keeping back of them a piece so she can cut in should she be needed," Dusty guessed. He had no way of knowing just how wrong the statement was. Then, glancing at Jones, who had sat down at the desk, he reached for the handle of the door. "Keep this shut and stay put unless you're needed. I'll go out and make talk with them."

"What do we do if they don't take to what you say?" McTavish inquired, looking through the left-side window and grasping the ten-gauge shotgun from the rack firmly.

"Whatever you have to," the small Texan replied. "Like I told the counselor, nobody gets lynched in *my* town."

"That's my sentiment all the way," the Scot asserted.

70

Going through the door and closing it behind him, Dusty crossed to the front edge of the sidewalk. Halting with his left shoulder against the post supporting the overhanging section that offered protection against the elements, he hooked his thumbs into the center of his gunbelt and looked about him. A number of people were coming from the nearby businesses. However, he was pleased to observe that none joined the crowd of men approaching along the center of the street. Nor, however, did they proceed in his direction. In one respect, he was pleased by that. The last thing he wanted was for somebody, no matter how well-intentioned, to make what could be interpreted as an attempt to halt the approaching crowd by force. To do that would almost certainly result in wholesale gunplay.

Returning his full attention to the approaching men, Dusty could not see a rope being carried by any of them—although he knew one could be procured easily enough should the mob get their way and fetch out the prisoner. He also noticed that the loafers and men from out of town were contriving to put the respectable local members of the group into the forefront and that these men looked apprehensive—a sure sign that a dangerous situation was developing. He was aware of the reputation he had built up as a peace officer who would take no sass where the enforcement of his duty was concerned. This, backed by the equal renown he had acquired from his ability to handle firearms and fight without weapons should the need arise, was certain to give pause to anybody contemplating going against him.

From his observations, the small Texan felt sure that the matter could be resolved without the need for recourse to measures sterner than a display of readiness. There were respectable young men present who would listen to reason and see the danger of trying to force their intentions upon the local law-enforcement officers. They would realize that his deputies were positioned where they could back him up most effectively. And should they discover that Calamity Jane and her freight-driver companions were in the vicinity they would be even more inclined to let the matter drop.

Dusty wondered where the redhead might be, since he could see no sign of her and felt sure he would have by now if she was behaving as he hoped would prove the case. Although she might strike some people as being irresponsible, he had never found her that way. Rather, she had always behaved in a most satisfactory manner whenever there had been the need for her to do so. However, there was no time to spend wondering why she had failed to put in an appearance.

"Would you gents have something in mind?" the small Texan inquired without moving from his position as the group came to a halt in a rough half-circle in the center of the street before the jailhouse. His tone continued almost gentle as he went on, "Or are you having a parade in honor of Flora McDonald's birthday?"

"It's not *that,* Captain Fog," the foremost member of the assemblage replied. Tall and slim, Dusty recognized him as Wendell Debutson, who, although they had not had much contact after an interview following Dusty's appointment as sheriff, Dusty knew was the only reporter for the *Spanish Grant County Herald*. At the moment, it was clear he did not relish having been put in the position of spokesman. "We all feel that Robin Harman and Cuthbert Castle should be brought to trial for their part in killing Toby Canoga."

"And who says they aren't going to be?" the small Texan inquired when the low rumble of agreement had died down.

"We mean *here* in Child City where it happened," Debutson elaborated. "Not by some federal court with a fancy lawyer to plead his case and a jury who didn't know Toby nor are likely to care about him being murdered the way he was."

"That's not the way the law says it has to be done," Dusty pointed out. "And Counselor Sutherland would tell you so, was he here."

"There's some's don't see it that way!" a voice yelled from among the crowd, but the speaker took care not to allow himself to be identified.

"There *always* is," the small Texan admitted, still with a mild timbre in his drawl. "And they just as always make sure they're standing where they can't be picked out as saying so."

"Nobody can say as Garve Sinjun's scared to be picked out!" yelled the big, burly red-haired young man who was the only son of the town's butcher, stepping forward until he was ahead of Debutson. Dusty knew him to have been one of Toby Canoga's closest friends, and also to have a quick temper when drinking. "I'm saying as how we aim to take

Harman and Castle so's the counselor can hold court on 'em and let their necks be stretched."

"That's not the way the *law* says it has to be done," the small Texan replied, straightening up. Not only his demeanor changed, but his voice took on a hard and warning intonation that those who knew him well recognized as a stiffening of resolve. "And, as long's I'm wearing this badge, I'm going to see the said law is obeyed. The only way you'll take *my* prisoners anywhere is by passing *me*."

On the face of it, for a man Dusty's size to be delivering these defiant words might have been considered highly ill-advised.

Except that at the moment, none of the crowd thought of the dusty-blond Texan as being small.

Every man present knew the reputation of the man whom they were facing. Those who had been in Child City for more than a few days were aware that he had defeated six would-be assailants with his bare hands at the Arizona State Saloon and killed two out of five men who had tried to capture Margaret Hart, driving the rest away. They might have the advantage of numbers in their favor, but the big Texan was sufficiently fast and accurate with his Colts to take more than one of them out should it come to shooting. In addition, they could see two figures holding shotguns at the partially open windows of the jailhouse and knew these would also be used against them if the need arose.

Concentrating his whole attention on the crowd, Dusty failed to see what was happening beyond them. Carrying a Winchester, a man in range clothes had gone up the stairs leading to a door on the second floor of the house at the left side of the alley across the street. However, he did not enter the building. Instead, standing on the small porch at the top, he brought the weapon to his shoulder and lined it over the heads of the group toward the spot where the small Texan was standing.

7
UP THE STAIRS, DUSTY!

At about the same time that Dusty Fog was preparing to deal with the mob and the attempted ambush of Mark Counter were taking place, events that they would have found of considerable interest were occurring in two Arizona towns.

★ ★ ★

"Howdy, Miz Maisie," greeted the elderly man whose skill as a telegraphist had, along with the influence of Colonel Myles Raines, obtained him the post of depot agent for Wells Fargo in Backsight. Holding out a buff-colored message form, he cackled, "Looks like this Edward Marsden jasper who sent this don't know as how you stopped being Mrs. Simons 'n' become Mrs. Randal when you married up with Biscuits."

"That's not all," the attractive woman who was co-owner of the Bismai restaurant remarked

75

after reading the information. She ran the dining-room side of the business while her husband employed the skill at cooking that had resulted in his sobriquet. "He doesn't know Miss Sue Ortega became Mrs. Sue Blaze when she was misguided enough to marry that fire-topped fugitive from Ole Devil Hardin's floating outfit. I must let Charles Henry and Marvin Eldridge know they aren't to expect being able to get a job on a ranch in Spanish Grant County. Can you find me somebody to take a message out to the Colonel's place, please, Saul?"

"Easy enough," the elderly man replied, although he suddenly realized that he could not remember having heard of the two men mentioned as being members of Colonel Raines's ranch crew. "Are you *sure* them's the feller's wanted?"

"I am," Maisie Randal stated. "And I'm sure they will be too."

★ ★ ★

"You gents wouldn't be playing all slick 'n' sneaky on a poor uneddicated country boy like me, now, would you?" Jack Straw inquired in a less-than-friendly fashion as he entered the sitting room of the house where the three conspirators still remained. "I thought we was going to leave the spreads up to Spanish Grant County to get their roundup done peaceable, seeing as how the kind of warriors as you call 'em don't take too kind to having to work as hard as is needed for such."

"What do you mean?" Willis Norman

76

growled, not caring for the implications of what the leathery-faced hired gun was saying.

"I ran across a couple of fellers who I figured would be just what we need up there," Straw explained, having crossed to the side-piece and helped himself to a drink of whiskey and a cigar without asking permission, as he always had in the past. "Only, when I asked if they'd take on for me, I'll be switched if they didn't say as how they'd already been hired to go up there 'n' help make fuss between the local spreads."

"I haven't hired anybody!" Anthony Blair asserted, and glared at the other two conspirators in quick succession. "Have *you*?"

"I haven't!" Norman claimed.

"Not *me*!" Graeme Steel affirmed in the same breath.

"Well, if we haven't," Norman rumbled, "who the hell has?"

"I wasn't told," Straw answered, the question having been directed his way. "And, being raised polite 'n' proper where such is concerned, I didn't ask."

"Can't you find out who it is?" Blair inquired.

"Maybe," the hired gun answered. "It'll likely run to money, though."

"How much?" Norman wanted to know, his tone bitter.

"Give me a hundred simoleons for starters," Straw demanded, extending his upturned left palm. "I'll let you know how much more it'll come to when I've found out."

While walking toward a saloon where he felt sure he would find the kind of men who could supply him with the information he sought, the hired gun saw a pair of Texans with whom he had no desire to come into contact. However, they were on the other side of the street and he assumed he had avoided their notice. He would not have been pleased if he had discovered how wrong his assumption was.

"Know that *hombre* over there, Lon?" Kiowa Cotton inquired, making an almost imperceptible inclination of his head in the direction of the hired gun.

"Can't say as how I've had me the pleasure," the Ysabel Kid answered, glancing at Straw in an equally surreptitious fashion. "If it'd be a pleasure."

"Not all that pleasurable, if he was working on another side from you," the savage-faced Texan drawled. Nothing in his expression or voice gave any indication of his feelings, or needed to where his companion was concerned. "I've seen him a few times hither 'n' yon. Called hisself Jack Straw last time, 'n' they do say he rates pretty fair as a hired gun. I've heard it said as he's no slouch on the draw with the short 'n' on the right and can throw lead from t'other, being a Cavalry Model, near to as good as most folks'd be with a carbine up to around thirty yards."

"And that land agent *hombre* who was all set to tell us what we wanted to know was some *closer'n* that," the Kid estimated. "And said Mr. Straw looks like he could Injun up on a couple of tired ole part-Injun boys like us was then without being heard, seen, nor even smelled. What say we find some place we can have words with him?"

"Best drop by 'n' see Stone 'n' the Major

first," Kiowa suggested. "So as they'll know what to say should the local John Law come asking what we've been doing."

The suggestion proved to have merit. On joining the boss of the Wedge and Major Wilson Eardle, the two members of General Ole Devil Hardin's floating outfit were told of the telegraph message from Child City. While agreeing that Jack Straw was worth investigation, the ranchers said they would feel more easy in their minds if one of the pair was to return to Spanish Grant County as soon as possible.

"You head out, Lon," Kiowa submitted. "None of my hosses can go near' as fast as your ole nigger hoss 'n' relay, way you'll likely be riding even effen it'll only be like a Comanch' and not one of us *real* hoss-Injuns. So you'll most like' be able to make some better time."

"Was I a suspicious man, which nobody can right truthful true say I'm *not*," the Kid replied, "I'd reckon you're just saying that so as you can have a few more days 'round town a-drinking 'n' a-carousing."

"Would I do *that*?" Kiowa challenged as if such a thought were repulsive to him. "I'm going to see if Mr. Jack Straw 'n' me can get sort of acquainted good enough for him to tell me what we're all wanting to know."

The plan was to come to nothing. Having been unable to acquire the information he required in Prescott, Straw told the conspirators of his plans and, claiming another fifty dollars for what he called traveling money, set off for Child City about three hours after the Kid had departed. However, he was not rid-

79

ing a relay and and therefore proceeded much more slowly than the baby-faced black-clad Texan, who traveled after the fashion of a Pehnane Comanche Dog Soldier warrior.

★ ★ ★

Having attained a position that would allow him to fire his Winchester Model of 1873 rifle so the bullet passed over the heads of the crowd and reach the man at whom it was being aimed, Nicholas Fay was prepared to earn his pay. When told who his victim was to be, he had had qualms over accepting the job. But he knew the distraction provided by the lynch mob would be certain to have the desired effect, and he had seen how he might do his job without any risk.

A younger hired gun might have relished the prospect of becoming known as the killer of Dusty Fog, but Fay was aware that what few benefits might accrue from this fame would be more than offset by the disadvantages. When word of how the Rio Hondo gun wizard had met his end got out, there were any number of men who would be determined to catch up with the responsible party. They all had reputations to chill a thinking man, but the Ysabel Kid would be worse than all the others combined. Fay decided that the only way to handle the affair was to carry out the assignment and, having collected the money he had been offered, put as many miles between himself and Spanish Grant County as possible.

The hired gun had left his horse tied to a

hitching rail behind the building whose stairs he had climbed to locate his target. All he had to do was make sure of his aim, squeeze the trigger, and return to his horse to ride away as fast as he could induce the animal to move.

Before cradling the butt of his Winchester against his right shoulder, Fay had raised and set the Sporting Leaf Rear Sight for one hundred yards, although the distance to his intended victim was less. With the weapon held securely in position for firing, he aligned the spikelike Sporting Front Sight in the center of the V-shaped notch on the raised scale at the rear so that it covered the chest of the small Texan standing outside the jailhouse. All he needed to do, the hired gun told himself mentally, was touch off the shot; he was confident enough in his ability as a marksman to be sure he would make the hit. Satisfied on that vitally important point, he began to apply pressure on the trigger.

At that point, there was a development that the hired gun had not anticipated.

"Up the stairs, Dusty!" a feminine voice screeched from somewhere not too far away, below and to the rear of where Fay was standing.

* * *

Calamity Jane and Steffie Willis had been all too aware that the way they had tried to counteract the damage to their attire before leaving the scene of the fight left much to be desired, and the scrapes and bruises on their faces was sure to arouse curiosity in anybody

81

the women encountered. So they had been relieved when they came into sight of the buildings flanking the main street without having met or—as far as they knew—been seen by anybody. Once across the street, they could go into the jailhouse and ask the ash-blonde's husband to fetch them more accept-able garments.

However, as the redhead and Steffie were approaching the alley through which they meant to pass, they saw a man with a rifle enter and start to climb the stairs. He had not looked in their direction, and his behavior struck them both as suspect. Continuing to advance, with Calamity drawing and cocking her Navy Colt as a precaution, they were able to see what was happening on the street in front of the jail-house. Both of them had had enough experience in the West to guess that the gathering was not for any peaceful purpose.

The redhead suddenly realized what Fay was preparing to do. With Calamity, to think was to act, and she yelled a warning to the small Texan.

The way in which Calamity alerted Dusty to the danger proved more efficacious than she anticipated. Hearing her shout—and he would have needed to be deaf not to—Fay could not resist the impulse to look around. Doing so caused him to involuntarily complete the pressure on the trigger and set the firing sequence in motion, while inadvertently allowing the barrel to stray a trifle from its align-ment.

It was just enough to ruin the hired gun's intentions.

Dusty had had no difficulty identifying the voice that alerted him, and he glanced past the crowd in the direction from which it had come. The sight of the man with the rifle caused him to react with the speed for which he was famous. Even as the bullet passed just over his head, his hands crossed in a flickering blur and each brought the bone-handled Colt Peacemaker from the carefully designed holster on the opposite side of his gunbelt. His forefingers did not enter the trigger guards, and the hammers remained uncocked until the barrels were turning outward and away from his body.[1]

"Kill *anybody* who tries to come in, Rusty!" Dusty commanded in a bellow that Silent Churchman of the Wedge, renowned for the volume of his voice, would have been hard put to equal. Then he sprang from the porch with his weapons ready for immediate use. "Tell Thorny the same!"

"Yo!" the stocky Wedge cowhand replied from inside the sheriff's office. "Count on Mac and me for *that*!"

"Aye, that you can!" Angus McTavish concurred from the other window. "Even though I might lose some good customers, and it being Flora McDonald's birthday to boot!"

Probably the comments were not heard, or made no impression on the assembled men, for they had something closer and more pressing demanding their attention.

1. How dangerous failure to take such a precaution when drawing and shooting a handgun could be is described in THE FAST GUN.

Every member of the crowd was taller and heavier than the small Texan. Some even fancied themselves as being wild, woolly, full of fleas, and never curried above the knees. However, seeing the way Dusty was behaving, not one thought of him in mere feet and inches. Nor was this response solely accounted for by the speed with which the twin Colts had come from their holsters. As had often happened in the past, the sheer force of his personality gave him the appearance of being the biggest man present. Far better to walk up to and slap the nose of a *ladino* longhorn bull, or tangle with a grizzly bear sow accompanied by her cubs than be foolish enough to try to block the passage of that *big* blond gun wizard from Rio Hondo County. With that in mind, they scattered to allow him an unrestricted way through so he could deal with whoever had tried to kill him.

"What the hell're you *doing*?" Rusty snapped, swinging his gaze around from where he was watching Dusty crossing the street as he heard the unmistakable click of a firearm's hammer descending upon either an empty chamber or a cartridge that failed to detonate.

"I thought one of those men was pulling a gun," Counselor Nigel Jones answered, working the lever of the Winchester 1873 rifle he had fetched from the rack on the wall when he had found it did not hold any more shotguns.

"There was nay the one that I could make out," McTavish asserted from the other side of the window to where the attorney was positioned.

"And none of 'em has, or at least if one did,

84

he's not tried to use it yet," Rusty growled. Relieved when nothing happened to suggest there would be an attempt to shoot Dusty, he went on. "Which there's no use trying to cut loose with that Winch. We keep only the scatters ready loaded on the rack."

Knowing something of such matters, the Wedge cowhand was all too aware of what would have happened had Jones fired into the crowd regardless of what had motivated him to do so. Every member of it who was armed would have started throwing lead at the jailhouse in response to what they would have considered the threat of further shooting from within. Then the violent confrontation the small Texan had been trying to avoid would erupt in all its fury and cause a number of needless deaths.

Recollecting the previous occasions when they had come into contact, Rusty was also surprised that the lawyer had even collected the rifle much less offered to use it in Dusty's defense. The only conclusions the Wedge cowhand could draw for it happening was that Jones had a higher regard for the upholding of law and order than might have been expected, or was determined to protect the life of the men being held in the cell and who were his clients.

In the alley, Calamity did not wait to decide what the man on the stairs might decide to do. Instead, grasping the butt in both hands and raising the Colt to shoulder height at arm's length, she lined its barrel in his direction. Seeing this happen, Fay found himself on the horns of a dilemma. Despite the battered condition of her face, the redhead handled the weapon in a way that suggested she was fully conversant with what she was doing and could pose a serious threat to him. Nor did the danger end there, the man he had been paid to kill was unharmed and, he did not doubt, would already be taking offensive action of a most effective kind. Sure enough, the small Texan had armed himself and was springing from the sidewalk.

The hired gun knew that he must take some kind of action in his own behalf and quickly. However, the problem was deciding what to do for the best. Concluding that the redhead would pose the lesser threat regardless of how competently she was holding the Colt, he began to turn the Winchester her way. As he did, showing no hesitation or suggestion of being perturbed by the danger, Calamity fired. In spite of her physical condition being weaker than usual, her excellent physical condition taken with well-developed feelings of self-preservation ensured she did not allow the weapon to waver.

Nevertheless, excellent though it was in many ways, the construction of the kind of revolver held by the redhead did not offer the better means of sighting available with the Winchester rifle Fay was using. Taking aim between the small notch in the tip of the cocked back hammer and small pin at the front end of the seven-and-a-half-inch octagonal barrel, as well as she could with the restricted vision resulting from the fight she touched off a shot. Flying as roughly as directed, not unexpectedly at such a distance even had she possessed her full sight, she missed her intended mark.

86

However, she was so close to achieving her purpose that one of the splinters kicked up by the .36-caliber bullet impacting against the wall of the building struck Fay on the cheek. Unfortunately, the slight prick from it did nothing to come even close to rendering him *hors de combat.*

Seeing Dusty emerging through the crowd as its members scattered out of the way, the hired gun thought fast.

There was, Fay decided, only one possible way out of his dilemma.

"Stop there 'n' drop your guns, Fog!" the hired gun yelled, putting the lever through the reloading cycle as swiftly as the rifle's mechanism permitted and swinging away from the small Texan to point its barrel downward. "I'll drop *both* the women afore you or anybody else can stop me!"

8
IT MAY NOT BE OVER YET

"There wasn't anything on the jasper I downed to say who he was, or why he was after me," Mark Counter told April Eardle. "I'd reckon he was a hired gun and he'd got over a hundred dollars in his pockets."

Saying he would only be found some work by that right mean cuss from the Texas Big Bend country who was roundup captain instead of the always kindly, considerate, and gentle-talking Captain Fog, Dude had suggested that the blond giant take the gather of cattle back to the bunch ground while Dude waited with the corpse until horses could be sent out. Mark had declared that his companion could not possibly be thinking of the Captain Fog who had been their trail boss when they took the Rocking H herd to Dodge City in the face of a warning from Wyatt Earp that it not go there. But he had agreed with the proposal and had found no great difficulty in carrying it out.

Arriving where the roundup's yield were being held, the blond giant had found nothing he could object to or criticize in what was being done. In fact, he had been satisfied that Jimmy Conlin was handling the post of straw boss as Mark himself would have done in Dusty Fog's absence. But to anybody with less knowledge of such things, it might have appeared to be a scene of total confusion.

Three cowhands from the AW ranch and the Wedge's Silent Churchman were carrying out a specialized duty. With the help of trained cutting horses they had brought from the remudas of their respective spreads, they were roping and removing the animals that bore no marks of ownership. Where calves were concerned, the brand borne by the mother was announced so it could be recorded and ownership established. Each animal caught was dragged to where other men waited to throw it to the ground and tie its legs with pigging thongs. Nearby a couple of fires burned, and from them arose the smell of burning hair and flesh caused by the branding of animals. By mutual agreement, as a gesture of friendship every animal bearing the brand used by Cornelius MacLaine, whose property and stock Stone Hart had inherited, was given a vent that burned a line through the brand. The Wedge brand was then inscribed nearby.

The noise was indescribable. Calves blatted in wild alarm on being captured and dragged by the neck to the waiting branding crews, then objected even more loudly to the process that followed. Enraged by the treatment of their offspring, the mothers bawled in rage and tried to rush to the defense of suffering youngsters. Such actions could only be thwarted by mounted cowhands, since the semidomesticated longhorns, male and female, had no fear for a man afoot. There was the added accompaniment of bawls from steers deprived of testicles, and the deeper thunder from bulls of all ages trying to escape from the gather and resume their free-ranging ways, which of course caused more work for the riders. In this situation, even the mildest of the ranches' crew members were given to a flow of the usual profanity, and the utterings of others—Silent Churchman being especially noticeable above the rest—were close to inspired.

Mark was informed by Conlin that such language had been withheld in the early stages out of respect for the person performing the vital duty of keeping the tally book, in which was recorded the number of cattle branded so that each ranch owner would know how many were to be added to his total. Other details, such as animals from spreads outside the area, were noted so that the owners could be notified. The task of keeping the book was one of great responsibility, and whoever was selected must be a person of integrity and clerical ability. Because it did not require any great physical prowess—although the ability to move quickly in the event of a cattle charge was advisable—the job was usually the province of an older man.

However, on this occasion, the keeper of the tally book was a woman. There being few enough cowhands to perform all the other duties, April Eardle had volunteered her services. She had stated that she possessed the required knowledge of bookkeeping and had cheerfully asserted that she was sufficiently agile to keep clear of danger. Not one of the hands would have thought of questioning her integrity, even though her past as a worker in saloons had been brought into the open during her first visit to Child City.[1] Rather, they admired her for her many good qualities and her willingness to take on the task.

In her late thirties, April was a fine-looking woman. She had blond tresses tucked into the crown of one of her husband's black Burnside hats. Her mature, beautiful face was already suntanned. As she always put it when alone with Major Eardle or in the company of very close friends, she had been "saved from a life of sin"; still, this was far from an accurate description of the way she had earned her living, most of her career having been spent as a senior hostess and supervisor rather than an ordinary saloon girl. Still firmly fleshed from a program of exercise, her Junoesque figure was pleasing to the masculine gaze, even though it was now usually garbed in a far

1. How this happened is told in ARIZONA RANGE WAR.

less revealing fashion, without being blatantly risqué, than it had been before her marriage.

The blonde had selected what she thought to be the most suitable attire for her work. Saying what was good enough for Calamity Jane was good enough for her, she had a gaily colored bandanna loosely rolled and knotted around her neck, and her black riding boots would permit any rapid movement better than the more stylish shoes she wore with her feminine attire. Despite being of a less snug fit, her open-necked man's tartan shirt and new Levi's pants borrowed from a suitable-size cowhand did not entirely hide the hourglass contours of her physique.

April had very quickly established one thing after coming to the bunch ground. Seeing and hearing how constrained the cowhands were in their language, she had had them all called together by Conlin shortly after Mark and Dude rode away. Then she told them that she had probably heard as much profanity as they could utter at various stages of her career around saloons. Therefore, with the proviso that they grant her a similar license, they were free to "cuss all you goddamned like" within her range of hearing during the working hours ahead. The statement had been greeted with cheers and grins. However, she had noticed that not even the youngest of them deliberately sought to take advantage of her offer.

"I've heard such always insist on getting paid in advance," the blonde declared when Mark had given her a brief account of the attempted ambush. Her voice had something of a sultry tone, but it was never sexually provoca-

91

tive and had not aroused hostility from the "good" women of Child City. Rather, as with the male population and cowhands, she had succeeded in winning them over despite her past involvement in saloons. "That way they'll have traveling money should things go so wrong they have to take a greaser standoff and light a shuck."

"Why, sure," the blond giant concurred, showing no surprise at the blonde's use of range term for running away in a very hurried fashion. "Or they could have been sent for by Eisteddfod like we thought the others in Child City were, so figured to pick up some more cash by gunning me down and taking what I'm toting."

"Except I got the feeling that you and Dusty thought we were wrong in figuring that way about them," April pointed out.

"*Dusty* always did talk too much," Mark declared in a way that was intended to imply he was innocent of the charge. "Trouble being, he 'most always makes right good sense. Which same shows by some of the company he keeps."

"I've always thought he picked real well with the Kid, but it ran out on him in another direction," the blonde asserted with a pointed glance at the man she was addressing. Then she became serious as she went on, "So it might not be over yet?"

"It just might not at that," Mark said, also serious. "And I'm going to have to get word to him what's come off. He'll have to know, being county sheriff until Amon Reeves gets back to doing it. Thing being, shorthanded as we are all 'round, who should I send?"

"Steffie was going in to Child for Margaret," the blonde said. She had been taking advantage of her circumstances to sharpen the tally-book pencils with a penknife she had brought for the purpose. Closing the blade and dropping it into the right-side pocket of her Levi's, she put the pencils in the breast pocket of her shirt. "Only, she'll be gone already, as she was saying how much fun it would be to go in."

April would remember the last sentence when she later heard how Steffie had spent part of the visit and about the predicament in which she and Calamity had found themselves.

★ ★ ★

Hearing the demand made by the hired gun on the stairs outside the building ahead of him, Dusty Fog prepared to take action. Knowing Calamity Jane as well as he did, he knew she would try to do something to help him out of the dilemma. He was equally confident that she would try to make her move in a way that would cause her to be the object of the man's intentions.

Sure enough, letting out a yell of "Get the bastard, Dusty!", the redhead flung herself away from Steffie.

Even as the redhead moved, the ash-blonde showed an equal alacrity and grasp of the situation by diving in the opposite direction.

With his rifle aligned on Calamity as the more dangerous of his intended victims, Nicholas Fay was caught unawares by the speed with which she moved. He was just as surprised to see Steffie taking evasive action.

93

Swiveling his gaze in the direction of the street, Fay found that his problems were in no way restricted to the actions of the redhead and the ash-blonde. But before he could decide what to do, the matter was taken out of his hands in no uncertain fashion.

Acting on instinct, Dusty responded to the danger posed by Fay firing both of his Colt Peacemakers in rapid successive turns as he ran forward, sending each successive shot in a slightly different trajectory. Fay needed to swing his Winchester rifle around before he could cope with his assailant. Although none of the bullets being thrown his way from the street had struck him, he knew he was in a dangerous spot—and the danger now increased from another direction.

Bringing herself to a halt as soon as she realized what Dusty was doing, Calamity thumb-cocked and raised her Navy Colt in her double-handed and arm's-length grip. This time she did not care whether she hit or missed. Her only intention was to cause the man on the stairs to be unable to turn his full attention on Dusty and use the greater potential for accuracy offered by the repeater. The lead she discharged flew to good effect. Caught in the back as he completed his turn, the hired gun was prevented from so much as taking aim at the approaching Texan.

Even as Fay received the bullet from Calamity, two .45-caliber shots, propelled by a more powerful charge of powder, ripped into his torso from the front. The combined impacts of the bullets caused him to throw aside the rifle unfired. He twirled around, hit and burst through the guardrail of the stairs, and fell to the ground. On landing, he saw the man he had been hired to kill approach, but he was too wounded to attempt any kind of resistance.

"Goddamn it!" Fay gasped as the small Texan came closer warily. "The bastard said I'd get you *easy* with that bunch outside the jailhouse making what'd pass as lynching talk!"

"Who told you?" Dusty asked, knowing he had no need for further precautions against the man, who he could see was very near death.

Too near, it was quickly apparent. Fay gave a convulsive shudder, then went limp. Letting out a low sigh of disappointment, Dusty returned the Colts to his holsters, then looked to his rear. What he saw caused him no concern. Not one of the crowd who had brought him from the jailhouse was showing the slightest indication of taking advantage of the situation to storm the jailhouse. Rather, they were all staring, awestruck at the way Dusty had dealt with the problem presented by the man in the alley. Satisfied on that account, Dusty swung his attention in the other direction.

"Well, between you and Dusty, we got out of *that* all right, Calam," Steffie said with relief evident in her tone.

"Why, sure," the redhead agreed, but with less enthusiasm. "Now all we have to do is tell Dusty how we got to be here in the shape we are 'n' needed to be got out of it."

9
IT MEANS SHOOTING A PRISONER WHO'S TRYING TO ESCAPE

"All right, you bunch," Dusty Fog said, returning to confront the crowd of men still assembled on the street outside the jailhouse. Although he had replaced his two Colt Peacemakers, few of the men were willing to meet his gaze as he stood with feet spread apart and thumbs hooked into his gunbelt surveying them with a grim expression on his face. "After you've been down the alley and see if you can recognize the man I had to kill, I want to see every one of you headed for any place you fancy around town as long as it isn't *here!*"

"The right to free and lawful assembly—!" Wendel Debutson began, seeing several pairs of eyes turn his way as if in search of guidance, but his tone was uneasy.

"What I've seen happening here doesn't come close to being *lawful* assembly!" an authoritative voice boomed. "And, unless I see Captain Fog's *legal* order being obeyed, it won't be *free* for any of you. In my capacity of justice of the peace for Spanish Grant County, I'll hold court under the powers granted to me by Article Sixteen, Paragraph Four, Subsection Five of the Territorial Charter to try you for impeding free passage along a public thoroughfare and conduct likely to cause a breach of the peace. The penalty for those is a fine of fifty dollars, or twenty-one days in jail."

From what was said, the reporter and the rest of the generally law-abiding members of the group had no trouble identifying the speaker. Counselor Edward Sutherland was approaching, and it was obvious that he was in a far-from-amiable mood. A number of older members of the community who had until then remained in the background—and because of family or business ties, most of them would have preferred to remain so—were with him. Even those present who failed to recognize the attorney were impressed by his demeanor and the facility with which he quoted what they believed to be an actual statute.

"Which, as we don't have room inside for so many of you," Dusty went on, coming from the alley without showing the slightest indication of the pleasure he felt over the way in which the attorney was handling the situation, "I'll do what my cousin Red Blaze did one time when he was handling the law by hauling all who can't get in held in leg irons down to the corral at the livery barn while they're working out their sentences. Now, what's it going to be, go do what I told you or stand trial afore the justice of the peace here?"[1]

"I wouldn't have given you time off to go to a wake for Toby Canoga if I'd known you'd be doing something as stupid as *this*!" Jason Sinjun growled, eyeing his son Garvin in a cold

1. Told in Part Two, "Cousin Red's Big Chance," THE HARD RIDERS.

fashion. "And I want you down to the shop *now*."

"Same goes for you, Wendel," said the editor of the *Spanish Grant County Herald,* Jurek Wiazcek, in an Illinois accent that gave no suggestion of his Polish origins. Of medium height and thickset, he was a regular member of the hunting and fishing group to which Sutherland belonged and had been ready to bring a shotgun to the jailhouse if he had decided such an action was required. "Anybody who works for me reports the news. He doesn't try to help *make* it."

Other members of the crowd had also decided that they were engaged in an ill-advised venture. The young men employed in the town were aware that parents and employers were gathering with displays of annoyance, and none was in a position to show defiance. The same was true of the local and visiting loafers, few of whom had anywhere near fifty dollars to pay a fine. And they suspected that the blond Texan wearing the badge of county sheriff meant what he said about the way in which the sentence would be carried out.

"*Deputy* Willis," the small Texan called, satisfied that no mob action would be resumed, "tell *Deputy* Bush to 'tend to things inside and Mr. McTavish can spend the rest of Flora McDonald's birthday doing whatever Scottish folks do on it. When you've done that, take a couple of blankets from the cells with you and see if anybody knows the feller I shot."

"Yo!" Rusty Willis replied. He was puzzled by the call for blankets, since he had been too occupied with watching the crowd to see his wife and Calamity Jane at the far end of the alley, much less notice how they were dressed. Swinging a sardonic gaze to Nigel Jones, he said, "You can put the Winch' back on the rack, Counselor. It won't be needed now. As sure as sin's for sale in Cowtown, there won't be none of that bunch figuring on doing meanness to your clients now. Stay put, Thorny, and mind what *Cap'n* Dusty said you was to do if *anybody* tries to get in."

"I'll mind it, *amigo*," Thorny Bush answered. "Only, I'd sure as hell like to know what's happening out front where it sounds like all the fun's been had."

"I'll come in and tell you all about it, laddie," Angus McTavish promised, accepting the shotgun Rusty was holding in his direction. "Just as soon as I've put the scatters on the wall again. They won't be needed out here."

Amused by the fact that the owner of the Arizona State Saloon had collected only the pair of guns Thorny and the Scot had held, Rusty went to collect the blankets. He told the tall, gangling youngster that he did not know why the blankets were needed, but that he was not about to start asking the boss fool questions at the moment. Then, as he set off to carry out his duty, he was so startled by what he saw that he came to a halt before arriving at the body.

"What the hell—?" the stocky Wedge cowhand exclaimed, staring from his wife to Calamity and back.

"We'll tell you about it later," the redhead promised as she and Steffie Willis hurried forward to take the blankets. The women draped themselves in the blankets as she continued, "Something tells me as how Dus—*Cap'n* Fog won't take kind to things not being done *exactly* the way he wants 'em. I do declare he was spoiled something fierce when—"

"Something tells *me* he's going to be asking *you* a few things afore today's out," Rusty interrupted, and ran a cold glance over his wife. "And, the same counts between you 'n' me, Steffie."

The ash-blonde knew there was a time and place for everything, and her instinct warned that this was neither the time nor the place for the glib repartee she and her husband often shared. Instead, both she and Calamity set off for the shelter of the jailhouse as fast as their legs would carry them. A number of curious glances were directed at them by some of the local men, who had been intrigued by the way in which they were dressed, but the women's bruised faces quelled their impulse to ask questions.

Leaving Rusty to handle the identification of the hired gun lying dead in the street, and nodding his thanks to Sutherland and the other two men who had spoken out, Dusty returned to the jailhouse office. His gaze was cold and forbidding as he studied the two women there, and they both looked decidedly sheepish. Seeing them react in such an untypical fashion, he was hard-pressed to prevent his sense of amusement from showing on his face, despite everything that had happened.

"I'll be back as soon as Steffie 'n' me've got us some fresh duds, Dus—!" Calamity stated. Her usual breezy and assured manner was missing.

100

"You'll *both* stay put until I've finished making talk with the prisoners," the small Texan interrupted in the coldest and most grim tone he could manage. "Unless either of you need to have Doc Gottlinger 'tend to your hurts?"

"I'll manage," the redhead said, without any of her usual cheerfulness.

"I'll do right well without disturbing him," the ash-blonde concurred in a similarly abashed and penitent fashion.

"Then sit down quiet' and start thinking up some pack of lies to explain what you've been doing 'stead of 'tending to your duties, *Deputy Sheriff* Canary," Dusty commanded, but he had to exert all his strength of will to continue sounding angry. "And I'd start to doing the same ready for when you next see your better half, was I *you,* Mrs. Willis."

"Do you know something, Mrs. Willis," Calamity said in barely more than a whisper when the small Texan had gone into the rear portion of the building, followed by McTavish. "I don't reckon Sheriff Fog's anywheres near to being pleased about what you 'n' I've been doing, looking the way we do."

"I'm starting to get the same notion myself, Deputy Canary," Steffie admitted in a voice that was no louder.

"I sort of figured along them selfsame lines when you didn't ask who he was talking about," the redhead said. "I bet that's the first time you ever admitted out in the open as that useless Wedge cowhand you let have the honor of taking you to wife is your 'better half'."

"It *is,* and'll be the last," Steffie declared, although she felt uncomfortable over the disapproval Rusty had shown. "Only, right now I reckon we'd both best get to thinking about what we're going to say when Sheriff Fog comes back and starts asking the why-all of what we've been up to."

"There's only one thing we can do, being women of spirit," Calamity asserted. "Look him right spang in the eye with the light of righteous truth on our faces—and lie like hell!"

★ ★ ★

Dusty Fog looked at the two clearly frightened prisoners with cold eyes. Neither had the appearance of being the kind of man who would willingly become involved in murder and the attempted robbery of the Cattlemen's Bank. Nevertheless, under the dominance of Mrs. Harriet Harman, they had done so, and were now facing the consequences with a distinct lack of equanimity.

Of just over medium height, Robin C. Harman—the C. was an abbreviation of Cook—was slim and had a weak face that was not improved by a growth of untidy whiskers. Although his Eastern-style clothing was of a good quality, the garments were untidy and he had done nothing to set them right.

Tall, lean, and miserable of expression at the best of times, Cuthbert Castle had unprepossessing features that were even more so in his present circumstances. He still had on his ill-fitting blue uniform he wore to identify himself as the armed guard for the bank premises, but he had not been allowed to retain his gunbelt and revolver.

"You know what's been happening out there, don't you?" Dusty asked.

"N-no—!" Harman answered, and Castle shook his head vehemently.

"I didn't reckon they *should* be worried none, all things considered, Cap'n Fog," Bush stated cheerfully. He was still sitting on a chair by the doorway into the office and nursing the ten-gauge shotgun he carried in addition to the two ivory-handled Colt Civilian Model Peacemakers in the cross-draw holsters of his gunbelt.

"And you didn't reckon *right,*" the small Texan declared. "It wouldn't have made them feel any too comfortable to know there was a mob outside yelling lynch rope and figuring to make them guests of honor at a strangling jig."

"You've stopped them!" Harman croaked. "Haven't you?"

"*This* time," Dusty confirmed with a chilling sense of certainty. "Though I don't know why the hell I bothered. They'll be coming back as sure as sin's for sale in Cowtown, and loaded for bear next time. Which, I don't see why me and my deputies should chance getting shot up for a couple of murderous sons of bitches like you." Dusty knew he was speaking merely to frighten the men behind bars.

"W-*we* didn't murder anybody!" Castle wailed. "It was all—!"

"Hell, you're only saying that 'cause she's dead and can't give the lie to it," the small Texan interrupted.

"It's your bounden duty to stop them!" Harman wailed, grabbing and shaking the bars of his cell with an intensity that turned his knuckles white under their grime. "You *have* to do it."

"Ain't none of us gets paid well enough to risk our necks for you pair," Bush put in. He had read correctly the brief glance sent his way by Dusty. "So Calam, Rusty, 'n' me are with Cap'n Fog in not figuring on doing it."

"We just might, 'though," Dusty commented, once again feeling satisfaction over the response from the rapidly maturing youngster, "was you to tell us who-all was behind you in running the bank and you had to try robbing it to stop them finding out how you've been cheating on them."

"Counselor Jones says I—*we* are only to answer questions when he's here to listen," Harman said sullenly. The response was mainly a result of his annoyance over how the small Texan had tricked him into believing he was seriously injured by the bullet his wife had fired to stop him from revealing their participation in the robbery at the bank. In fact, the bullet had been deflected by the watch in the right pocket of his vest and had left him with nothing worse than bruised ribs. "So you can send for him, as I'll only talk to you in his presence."

"Mr. Harman looks like he's needing to go out back, Deputy Bush," the small Texan drawled, hoping the youngster would continue astute. "Take him and let him do what he needs to do."

"Yo!" Bush assented, rising and taking the

104

key ring from the hook by the door. As he was crossing to unlock the cell that the banker was occupying, he called, "Come on out, *Mr. Harman.*" The need for Harman to answer the call of nature had made itself increasingly felt during the conversation, so the order was obeyed willingly. However, as they were going to the rear door, he continued, "Do that *ley fuega* as the greasers're said to do down to ole Mexico mean what I reckon it do, Cap'n Fog?"

"It *do*," Dusty agreed. He concluded that his confidence in the youngster's acumen had not been misplaced. "If you heard it means shooting a prisoner who's trying to escape, even though he might not be trying at all. Only, nothing like *that's* going to happen around here, is it?"

"Why, surely not," the youngster asserted, but his tone lacked conviction.

Thorny opened the back door and shoved the banker through it with the muzzles of his shotgun.

"Wha—Wha—?" Castle gurgled. He heard a startled exclamation from his brother-in-law before the door was closed and the key clicked in the lock from the outside.

"Maybe *you'd* like to answer for me?" Dusty inquired.

Before the scared former guard for the bank could speak, he heard a disturbance outside the rear of the building.

"Halt!" Bush could be heard yelling after a crash from the shotgun. "Halt, else I'll have to shoot you down!"

10
WHO-ALL WAS BEHIND YOU?

"Wh—wha—what's *happened* out there?" Cuthbert Castle howled, and instead of waiting for an answer, he flung himself toward the barred window of the cell to stand on the bunk and look out.

"Get down off there!" Dusty Fog snapped. He jerked open the door and, making sure the skinny former guard of the bank had time to see Robin C. Harman lying sprawled facedown with Thorny Bush standing holding his smoking shotgun, hauled him away from the window. "Goddamn it, that's civic-owned 'n' -paid-for property you're standing on."

"He—he k-k-k-!" Castle croaked as he was shoved toward the front of the cell with a force he would not have expected from so small a man.

"What happened, Dusty?" Calamity Jane asked. She had discarded the blanket before coming from the sheriff's office, holding her Navy Colt and moving with an alacrity that was clearly giving her bruised body some pain.

"Thorny just shot something," the small Texan replied in a harsh voice, looking in what Castle interpreted as defiance from the redhead to Angus McTavish and back.

"Those things happen, even on Flora McDonald's birthday," the Scot commented dryly. He had drawn the same conclusion

Calamity had, and he wanted to help create the desired impression on the obviously terrified remaining prisoner. "Does your man need any help back there, Captain Fog?"

"He'll yell if he does," Dusty said. "Go back to the office and don't let anybody else in for a spell. There could be some more gunplay soon."

"You want for Steffie 'n' me to stay, D— Cap'n Fog?" the redhead inquired, her tone showing that an answer in the negative would be appreciated.

"You're damned *right* I do," the small Texan growled. He felt that his female deputy deserved to be taught a lesson in responsibility, and was sure Rusty Willis would have the same idea with respect to the ash-blonde. "I don't reckon I'll be long, then I've a few things I want to say to you pair."

Turning around without another word, Calamity followed McTavish's lead in carrying out the instructions. They had just returned to the office when the front door was thrown open and the stocky Wedge cowhand came in, followed by Wendel Debutson and a few other townspeople.

"What's up, Calam?" Rusty inquired without as much as a glance at his wife, who was standing by the weapon rack, her blanket discarded, and taking down a shotgun. He continued coldly, "Leave it be and cover yourself up, Steffie!"

"Thorny went out to the backhouse and took him a shot at a chicken hawk," the redhead replied, saying the first thing that came to her mind.

"Does Dusty want me?" the Wedge cowhand asked as Steffie began carrying out the order with a speed that suggested a guilty conscience.

"You'd best go see," the redhead advised.

"Excuse me, ladies," Debutson said after Rusty had gone into the cell section and closed the door, McTavish stepping to lean against it. Rusty had hoped the shot might produce a different story, but he concluded that this would not be the case. "But who gave you those black eyes?"

"Nobody *gave* us them!" Calamity said.

"They damned well *didn't,*" Steffie agreed, taking her cue quickly. "We had to *fight* like hell for them."

"Only, don't ask us who we was fighting," Calamity warned, oozing a seeming menace that the ash-blonde duplicated. "'Cause that's *our* business 'n' none of your own."

Behind the jailhouse, Bush was delivering an explanation for the shotgun blast in a way that supported the redhead's contention.

"It's all right, folks," the youngster was saying, holding down his voice to avoid being heard through the glass panes of the cell's window. "I was taking this gent to the backhouse when I saw me a chicken hawk going over. Damned if when I up and cut loose at it, he didn't just swoo him a swoon from fright."

Doctor Klaus Gottlinger walked forward to carry out an examination of the unmoving figure lying facedown at Bush's feet. He stated that he was satisfied Harman was only unconscious and had not been shot, but he refrained from mentioning one thing he noticed.

There was a bump on the back of the banker's head that could not have been caused by landing in that position.

* * *

"All right, *hombre*," Dusty Fog growled, holding Cuthbert Castle pressed backward against the door of the cell and contriving to put a mean timbre in his voice. "Do *you* want to sit around waiting for his attorney to be on hand afore you answer a few questions?"

"H-he's *my* attorney as well!" the scrawny young man pointed out.

"That surely isn't the way it sounded to me, since Counselor Jones come here and said he was acting for *Mr. Harman*," the small Texan claimed with the same chilling menace. "He's never even *once* mentioned you as being his client. So, after what's just happened to Harman, I don't conclude he'll give shit, spit, nor piss in the bucket should the same get done to you."

"Wh-Why should it be done to me?" Castle gasped. "It was *Harriet,* not *me,* who killed Canoga and shot Sheriff Reeves."

"There were some fellers out front reckoned as how you 'n' Harman both was just as much to blame and wanted to have you dangling from a cottonwood," Dusty replied, continuing to employ ungrammatical speech as an aid to creating the kind of character he wanted the prisoner to believe him to be. "With Counselor Jones acting for *him* and Counselor Sutherland as justice of the peace to hand, me 'n' my boys had to do something. Those fellers have gone, but they'll be coming back for another stab at it once they've took on some more bottled brave-maker, sure as sin's for sale in Cowtown. I don't see as how *we* should have to stick our necks out *twice* trying to hold 'em off, 'specially when there's a right easy way of getting 'round it should we do that greaser *ley feuga* 'n' shoot you trying to escape."

"Rob— He wasn't trying to escape!"

"*You* know it 'n' *I* know it, but that's how it's going to look 'n' be told when folks come asking why-all he got made wolf bait. Which same'll apply just as good should we do it to *you*."

"You *daren't* do the same thing again!" Castle yelped.

"We're not loco enough to pull it that way twice," Dusty countered. "Way it'll be set up, you'll've got windows put in your skull 'cause you tried to jump my deputy when he let you out of your cell 'cause you allowed you wanted to go out back."

"Nobody will believe *that*!" the skinny prisoner tried to state emphatically, but the words came out with no conviction whatsoever.

"They sure as hell *will*," Dusty asserted. "Being good friends of Toby Canoga 'n' tax-paying citizens to boot, they'll all say right has been done by him and it saved the county the cost of a trial 'n' hanging. Shucks, I'll bet Counselor Jones'll be right pleasured that he won't get asked to speak out in your defense, 'specially seeing as how he wasn't hired 'n' paid to do same in the first place."

To say Castle was terrified would be an understatement.

On being sent to college, having found himself to be completely devoid of the intelligence that his doting middle class-middle management parents had always led him to assume he possessed, Castle had joined others of his kind in adopting liberal pretensions in an attempt to conceal his inadequacies. One of the concepts that he had embraced was a paranoiac hatred of Southerners. He had been led to believe there was nothing vile and reprehensible that those who lived south of the Mason-Dixon line would eschew.

Now Castle found himself at the mercy of a man who had first attained fame fighting for the Confederate States—a man who, moreover, a short while earlier had—according to a member of the group who shared his political beliefs—viciously attacked them in the Arizona State Saloon without any provocation, then threatened to kill them on sight unless they left Child City.[1]

Furthermore, he had just allowed Harman to be taken out and shot under a false pretense. Castle remembered that the shout for his brother-in-law to halt was made *after* the shot was fired. The killing had been carried out with the knowledge and consent of the blond Texan who was now threatening him, and he did not doubt that he would be accorded the same treatment.

"Are you ready to start answering some questions?" Dusty asked, satisfied he had created the desired effect. "Or do you want to head for the backhouse. Only, you won't get

1. The incident is described in WEDGE GOES TO ARIZONA.

111

all the way there, seeing as Thorny only used one shell from his scatter and it allus holds two." Heading off an interruption from Castle, he continued, "Which I don't reckon as how Counselor Jones'll be too all-fired worried over it happening, seeing's how he won't be able to get him no more fees for his services and'll know what siding with you, 'specially with his client dead, will do to his chances of setting up here as a law-wrangler like he's aiming to do. No sir, even if it hadn't already been decided to throw you to us wolves, he'll care even *less* about it when he hears you've wound up wolf bait as well. 'Course, was you to tell me something useful about what really come off at the bank, I'd just natural' have to keep you alive to repeat it afore the counselors."

The small Texan possessed a sound judgment of human nature and had selected what he believed the most suitable way of trying to obtain the information he was seeking. This went beyond who had murdered Toby Canoga and seriously wounded the sheriff. His every instinct told him that there were motives and factors that had not yet come to light, and he was hoping to hear something to verify that belief.

"Wha—What do you want to know?" Castle groaned.

"Who-all was behind you bunch at the bank?" Dusty asked. With no more apparent effort than if he were dealing with a tiny child instead of a man, he swung the prisoner around and propelled him to land sitting on the bunk. " 'Cause I figure none of you stacked high 'nough to be chiefs 'n' was just li'l Injuns taking orders from them as was chiefs."

"I don't know what you *mean,*" Castle asserted in a desperate attempt to bluff.

"It's this *simple,*" the small Texan said in the same threatening manner. "Who-all was behind you?"

"I don't *know!*" Castle yelped, growing more alarmed. "Honest to God, I don't. Harriet and Rob never told me *anything* about what they were doing."

"But a right sneaky li'l son of a bitch like I figure you to be would find some way of finding out," Dusty assessed. "Even if it meant listening at a keyhole while him 'n' her was talking private together in bed of a night, 'stead of doing what decent folks'd be doing. So what did you hear?"

"Nothing!"

"*Nothing?*"

"All I ever heard was Rob complaining that she never told *him* anything of what was going on. He told you at the bank that she was the one who'd arranged and done everything that happened."

"Why, sure," Dusty drawled in a mocking tone of disbelief. "Why *wouldn't* he tell me that. His missus'd just been gunned down by Calamity Jane and couldn't give him the lie on it, which he reckoned you'd be too yeller-bellied 'n' eager to save your own skin to do."

"It's the truth, so help me God!" Castle wailed. "You didn't know Harriet. She was always a vicious and domineering bitch. The last thing she'd do would be let either Rob or me know anything more than we needed to. All she said was that we were coming here to run the bank."

"Like hell," the small Texan sniffed, although a supposition he had drawn had been confirmed. "You three owned it."

"We *never* did!" Castle protested. "She came to tell us that Rob was to make like he did and play the banker."

"And all she'd let you do was be the guard," Dusty drawled. "A man could've got killed doing that if some bunch of owlhoots had come in to do the robbing from behind drawn guns, like most times happens out here."

"I know," the prisoner said bitterly. "But she insisted that was what I did. According to her, I'd be useless as a teller or anything else. I didn't care for it, but I did it as I've always done whatever she told me. Like I said, you didn't know her. She was the brains and made all the decisions. Rob was nothing more than a figurehead—and not a very good one, she often used to tell him."

"Supposing I believe you," the small Texan said. He was sure he was hearing the truth about the woman. She had struck him as being of a most domineering nature the first time they had met, and he had not subsequently found cause to change his mind. "Who-all was behind you?"

"I don't know!" Castle declared vehemently. "And it wasn't for want of trying to find out. All I learned was that *she* was working for some Eastern financiers, but wasn't able to get to know who they were and for what purpose they'd sent her here. If Rob wasn't dead, he'd tell you the same."

"Let's ask him, shall we?" Dusty suggested, then raised his voice and said, "Hey, Thorny, if Mr. Harman's done out back, fetch him in."

"Yo!" came the youngster's reply, and he pulled open the rear door to allow Harman to precede him into the cell area.

★ ★ ★

"And now, ladies!" Dusty Fog said in a grim tone, although he was inwardly amused by the sheepish way in which the pair he addressed were behaving as they took the chairs placed on the other side of his desk by Rusty Willis and Angus McTavish. The Scot had left the office, but Rusty had remained, and he stood leaning a shoulder against the wall at the rear of the office. "Just what kind of a game have you been playing?"

The sight of Robin Harman unharmed had caused Cuthbert Castle to begin talking. Dusty thanked the skinny prisoner for being so informative, even though everything had been laid at the doorstep of his brother-in-law. Castle had been taken by Bush for a needed visit to the backhouse and Harman had forgotten his earlier intransigence and sought to clear himself of the accusations immediately. However, he stuck to his assertion that his wife was to blame, and he said much the same about his relationship to her as his brother-in-law had. Studying him closely, Dusty had been convinced that he was too frightened by his experience outside to lie about the extent of his knowledge.

Satisfied that nothing further could be learned from either prisoner, the small Texan had ordered Harman returned to the cell, then left them in Bush's charge.

Returning to his office, Dusty was looking forward with amusement to dealing with Calamity Jane and Steffie Willis. From their expressions upon seeing him, he concluded that they did not share his enthusiasm. He had never seen the normally self-confident ash-blonde so subdued. And the normally ebullient redhead gave the impression that she wished she were anywhere in the world except there.

"I got this letter writ in what I figured was a gal's hand telling me as how she'd got something about what's going on hereabouts that *you'd* like to know and where to meet up," Calamity said without any of her normal verve. "Said I'd got to come alone, else she'd light a shuck and forget it. Only, when I arrived I found the gals from the cantina was waiting. One of 'em allowed as how I'd whupped her li'l sister someplace and she was looking for evens."

"How many of them were there?" Dusty asked. He had to force himself to keep his manner cold.

"Just the six," the redhead replied, still too perturbed to detect the small Texan's real feelings on the matter.

"Just the six?" Dusty growled. "So I suppose you concluded you could whup them all and started to try to prove it?"

"Wasn't that way at all," Calamity denied. "She said she'd take me on herself."

"And you believed her?" the small Texan queried sardonically.

"I figured she might be lying," the redhead went on in her own defense, "so I started in

116

to knocking her to where I'd left my gun 'n' whip, figuring I could get one or t'other to keep the rest of 'em off my back."

"Only, I came barging in before it could be done," Steffie put in, deciding the time had come for her to shoulder the blame. "Without waiting to be asked even. So it was all *my* doing that we had to take them on."

"If I hadn't gone there instead of—!" Calamity began, determined to avoid having the ash-blonde, for whom she had formed a great liking and respect, regarded as being at fault in any way.

"You didn't ask me even once to follow you and join in," Steffie objected. "It was my own idea!"

"Spare me all the 'I'm as much to blame as she is,' *please!*" Dusty requested, summoning all his self-control to retain his somberly disapproving pose. "I reckon you did what you figured was best when you got the message, Deputy Canary, and, coming on the scene by pure nothing else but accident, you allowed she needed help, so went in head down and horns a-hooking to give it, Mrs. Willis?"

"That's just how it was," Calamity declared.

"I couldn't've put it better myself," Steffie seconded. "And I think it's a poor thing if a deputy can't follow up something without needing to ask the sheriff if it's all right first. Besides, if we hadn't done what we did, we wouldn't've been at the alley in time to stop that feller shooting *you.*"

"Damned if I hadn't clean forgotten that," Dusty declared, and allowed his pose to start ebbing away as if reluctantly. "All right, I'll have to come right out and say you both acted for the best. Anyways, who won?"

"We did," the redhead stated. She didn't add "of course" verbally, although it was implied by her tone.

"I know we don't look that way," the ash-blonde supported. "But you should see *them*. They're a whole heap worse."

"But not as bad as they're going to feel when I go see them!" Rusty put in, and there was nothing false in his anger.

"Which you're *not* going to do, husband mine!" Steffie affirmed. "Not after we licked them fair 'n' square and they've said they accept it. So there's no way I'm going to let you—or you, Cap'n Fog—go making fuss for 'em."

"I'm with Steffie on *that*!" Calamity declared. "Hell, I could've backed water and held off with my whip 'n' gun, but didn't. So I'm willing to say it's over."

"Very well, seeing as how that's the way you both want it played," Dusty said. Then he rose and walked around the desk to thrust his right hand under the girl's kepi and gently ruffle her hair. "Goddamn it, gal, Mark was calling it right when he said you're a red-topped lump of perversity."

"Goddamn you, Dusty Fog!" the redhead yelled indignantly as realization struck home. "You've been joshing us poor suffering li'l gals all along."

"I figured you both deserved it," the small Texan drawled. "And, if I didn't before, I know now why folks call you Calamity."

11
WHO'S OUT THERE?

"Howdy, Cap'n Fog," Derek Hatton greeted, coming from the bar hurriedly when the small Texan entered the *cantina*—which still had not yet received an official name nor had been completely renovated—followed by Thorny Bush. Hatton's voice indicated that his origins were in Illinois. There was a somewhat worried expression on the sullen lines of his unprepossessing features. Of slightly over medium height, he had a thickset frame now running more to fat than hard muscle. Although there was a Colt Civilian Model Peacemaker revolver in the tied-down holster of his Western-style gunbelt, his attire was that of an Easterner with money but a bad sartorial sense. Gesturing to his partner behind the counter, he went on in an equally surly tone, "Steve and I've been expecting you."

Three inches taller than Hatton and lean to the point of gauntness, Steven Scott was no better-looking than his partner. His garb was that of a professional gambler, and there was a short-barreled Merwin & Hulbert Army Pocket Model revolver—its forward-pointed butt available to either hand—tucked into the scarlet silk sash around his waist. Although he was glowering at the two Texans, he made sure he did not do anything that might be construed as an attempt to draw his weapon.

119

The time was almost nine o'clock in the evening.

Nothing of note had occurred since a much-relieved Calamity Jane and Steffie Willis had been dismissed from the sheriff's office with advice from the small Texan to "go get dressed like decent womenfolks, even though one of you has never been *that* and I'm starting to have some doubts about the other no matter how good she might be at hauling out babies." Having recovered her usual spirits, the red-head had replied with a less than flattering description of "a certain varmint from Rio Hondo County who I'll leave nameless called Dusty Fog and who's a disgrace to Ole Devil's floating outfit and the whole danged Lone Star State." Also looking more like her normal competent and controlled self, the ash-blonde had stated that she intended to keep a more careful watch on who her loving husband played with in the future, since she did not want him getting bad habits.

Although Steffie had obtained clothing from Matilda Canoga—whose baby Steffie had delivered—to replace her ruined garments, she had not felt up to going back to the Wedge ranch house, and Dusty had said that Rusty could take the night off to be with her as guests in the home of Sheriff Amon Reeves and his wife Libby. After taking a hot bath at the Summers Hotel and changing into fresh clothes, Calamity had reported to the jailhouse to announce that she was ready to resume her duties as deputy. The old-timer who had served as turnkey for Reeves was still away on a fishing trip, and she had been told to take things easy by handling the duty, which Bush had performed most satisfactorily throughout the events of the afternoon. Still not feeling her best, although she would never have admitted it, she had been pleased to be given what they all believed to be a sedentary occupation.

Nobody had claimed to recognize the man who tried to kill Dusty. A search of his pockets produced no suggestion of his identity, nor did an examination of his belongings in the war bag from his bedroll on the horse he had meant to use for his escape after the shooting. Neither had the brand borne by the animal proved helpful. The horse came from a ranch in northern Arizona and had no distinctive features; nor was it of such a quality that it was likely to be remembered by the ranch's owner or any of the crew on that account. The small Texan knew the horse could have passed through several hands anyway, and he decided nothing could be learned by sending a telegraph message requesting information. In his opinion, all that had come out of their efforts was a further lesson for Bush on the routine work of a lawman.

Shortly before dark, Peaceful Gunn had arrived from the Wedge ranch house bringing the man killed by Mark Counter and a report on how the killing came about. Once again faced with having to make an identification, Dusty had realized that the condition in which the corpse arrived—so long after the killing—made easy identification unlikely. The only significant point to emerge was that the man brought in by the Wedge hand had coins in his possession similar to those found on the other dead man.

121

The small Texan was faced with a problem. Although he would have liked to go to the site of the ambush and see what could be learned there, he knew of nobody in town or on the roundup sufficiently skilled at tracking to determine where the ambushers had come from or where the survivor went. In addition, still uneasy over the mob incident in front of the jailhouse, he had no wish to leave town without a full force of deputies left behind as a deterrent to further mob activity. In the end, he had simply asked Peaceful to return and tell Mark to warn everybody at the Wedge and AW ranches, guards and roundup workers alike, to be alert for trouble.

Calamity was available, so Dusty had had Bush accompany him on a round of the town. He had left the cantina for last. Looking over the batwing doors, he had found—not unexpectedly, since the Arizona State Saloon was still closed "for Flora McDonald's birthday"—business thriving. He recognized a number of the men who had been outside the jailhouse, but they were scattered around the room and appeared to be relaxing rather than plotting further mischief. He had not been surprised by his discovery that a number of more prominent citizens—including McTavish, Counselor Edward Sutherland, and the other attorney—were present, knowing this to be a common courtesy when a new place opened in a town. None of the female employees were in evidence, but he had not expected that there would be.

"I figured we would drop in, seeing as we're

making the rounds," Dusty replied to the less-than friendly greeting he received on entering. "Things look to be going well tonight."

"We can't complain," Hatton replied, and after a glance toward Counselor Nigel Jones, he went on, "About this afternoon—!"

"What about this afternoon?" the small Texan queried. "Hell, you didn't know what those knobheads were fixing on doing when they came in here, and nobody can blame you for taking a chance to do some business."

"But—!" the stocky man began, looking as if he was expecting lightning to strike at any moment.

"Counselor Jones told me that you was figuring on closing down when you got wind of what was coming off," Dusty continued as if the interruption had not been made. "I'm obliged to you for that, sir."

"Yeah!" Hatton grunted. "But what about—?"

"The fuss that stopped you bringing your ladies in tonight?" the small Texan inquired, looking as if he had just realized what was disturbing the other man. "Way I was told, what came off between them and Calam was personal from something that happened to one of 'em's sister when they tangled in a saloon one time. She and Mrs. Willis both say most firm and determined they're well-satisfied with the way things turned out and aim to have things let ride. Like that loco red-topped gal I was crazy enough to take on as deputy pointed out, she wasn't on duty when it happened. So seeing as they feel that way about what came off, I don't reckon it's any of my nevermind as sheriff to butt in. Unless, of course, you or any of your ladies want it dealt with otherwise?"

"They *don't!*" Hatton stated, suspecting that any questioning of the battered saloon girls might reveal what had really caused the fight. "But Steve and me thought you'd come in—!"

"We've just dropped by on the rounds, like whoever's doing them'll be doing every night so long as we're here," Dusty drawled. "Right or wrong, what came off between the ladies is their affair and not the law's. Seeing as how they locked horns in the woods out there, the peace around the town wasn't broken." Then his voice took on a note of warning. "Only, that fuss had better be the end of it, and you make sure every one of your ladies knows that."

"I will," Hatton promised, knowing the threat was aimed at him rather than his female employees. Relieved to have got away with the incident so lightly, he decided that a friendly gesture in return was advisable. "Will you take something—to ward off the cold air, Sheriff?"

"I reckon a beer apiece for me and my deputy might just do that," the small Texan assented. He knew the gesture was a declaration that his warning had been noted and would be acted upon. Nodding in the direction of the table at which Sutherland was sitting, he continued, "I don't conclude our justice of the peace will object to just the one, seeing there's a nip in the air and it's Flora McDonald's birthday."

"I've been wondering about that all day,"

Hatton declared, making no effort to hide his relief at the way things had turned out. "Just who the hell is Flora McDonald?"

Before Dusty could reply, there was the sound of an explosion, followed a few seconds later by a revolver shot from somewhere in town.

Spinning around, as did Bush, the small Texan led the rush from the building. On emerging, they started to run in the direction from which the noise had come. As they arrived on the main street, they were able to tell where the explosion had occurred. Although the sheriff's office was now in darkness and showed no sign of damage from their position, already a number of people were hurrying toward it. Filled with concern for Calamity, the two Texans increased their pace to a full sprint. Passing through the citizens, they noticed that the windows of the jailhouse had been shattered.

"Calam!" Dusty yelled, shoulder-charging the front door open as if it were not there.

Once more displaying his coolness in an emergency, Bush had snatched the lantern from the hand of the butcher in passing to illuminate the scene in the jailhouse. Letting out an exclamation of thanks for the sturdy construction of the building, Dusty went to where the redhead was hoisting herself up slowly from the floor. She was obviously shaken up by what had happened and might even have added a couple of bruises to her already numerous collection, but she showed no indication of being seriously hurt.

"In—in the back!" Calamity gasped.

Going past the redhead and directing a

look of relief at her, Bush went through the burst-open door giving access to the cells. The light of the lantern allowed him to see that there was a big hole in the wall between the two cells used for holding Robin C. Harman and Cuthbert Castle. Both of the prisoners were lying motionless against the front bars, as if thrown there by the explosion that had caused the damage. Going closer, the youngster saw that the banker's injuries went beyond those he had sustained as a result of the blast, and also explained why a revolver shot had been heard. A bullet had passed through his head.

"Either he knew something he didn't let on to me," Dusty said, staring at Harman, "or whoever did this figured he might and made sure he couldn't tell it if he did."

★ ★ ★

Lifting his head and coming to his feet alongside his mistress's bed, the big Chesapeake Bay retriever that served as what a later generation would call a seeing-eye dog gave a low growl. Waking instantly, Margaret Hart leaned over to lay a hand on his rough coat and, swinging her feet to the floor, followed him to the window. Deftly running her fingers across the lower pane, she found the catch, unfastened it, raised the sash silently, and spoke in little more than a whisper.

"*Quiet,* Rollo. I hear them!"

If anyone who did not know her had seen the way in which Margaret was behaving, they would have never suspected she was blind. Five feet seven in height, she had curly

126

tawny hair and an attractive face. Her disheveled state was evidence of her just having been woken up. Beneath her plain dark-blue nightdress it was obvious that her build was far from bony or even slender.

In the short time she had been living at the ranch house that her husband had unexpectedly inherited from his uncle, Cornelius MacLaine, aided by Steffie Willis and the Mexican woman who had accompanied them from Texas, Margaret had already succeeded in becoming oriented to its furnishings and fittings. Therefore, she had experienced no difficulty in finding her way to the window to open it and try to ascertain the cause of Rollo's warning. While speaking to the dog, she collected the short-barreled, ten-gauge, British-made Greener shotgun originally produced for use by guards on Wells Fargo stagecoaches. Because of the troubles that had plagued them since their arrival, it was kept on the table ready for any emergency requiring the use of firearms.

Although the ash-blonde had not returned from Child City—she would have been in the small house supplied as living quarters for her and her husband anyway—Margaret was not alone in the house. After having kept the tally book for the roundup all day, April Eardle was sleeping in the guest room. However, Margaret had no wish to wake her— the warning given by Rollo might have been caused by nothing more than a prowling animal. Her acute hearing compensated for her loss of sight, and it soon told her that whatever had disturbed the big dog was definitely human. Furthermore, the stealth being

127

employed suggested that whoever was out there in the darkness was not engaged on a friendly mission.

Margaret was aware that none of the Wedge ranch's crew who had been left behind as guards would behave in such a furtive manner. Nor would either Rosita or Jose Martinez— the latter had taken on the duties of nighthawk due to the elevation of the Negro Tarbrush to wrangler for the ranch's *remuda*—be doing so even if they had some need to leave their accommodation. She was just as certain that anybody who had come in from the bunch ground for any reason would not be lurking around in this fashion. Most cowhands possessed a lively sense of humor, but they were also sensible enough to know that such behavior would not be considered amusing. After what had happened to Mark Counter and Dude that afternoon, this activity could even prove dangerous.

Margaret drew back the hammers of the shotgun with as little noise as possible. At that moment, the breeze carried a further warning that whoever was outside was not there for any legitimate reason: Her nose detected the smell of kerosene and she detected faint splashing sounds, as though some of the inflammable liquid was being scattered around.

But Margaret could not be sure of the intruders' exact location, and she knew she must not open fire until she was sure of where to aim the shots. She was also aware that, despite the risks to herself involved, she must take protective measures before she let her presence become known. A touch on the rump from her left hand caused the dog, which had moved by her side, to sink to a sitting position. Then she moved her fingers along the wall until she was satisfied that she was standing alongside and not in front of the window. Then, contriving to give her voice a harshly masculine timbre, she delivered the challenge she felt sure would achieve her purpose.

"Who's out there?"

As soon as the words where uttered, Margaret received the response she desired.

There was the crash of a revolver from the position where she had heard the approaching men, and the bullet came through the window. Showing judgment of direction similar to that used when she had guided Dusty Fog's aim as he was protecting her in the darkness against an attempted abduction on the night of her first visit to Child City, she turned the shotgun to the window and aimed it toward where she heard the hammer of the handgun being cocked. A gentle squeeze on the forward trigger caused the shell in the right-side barrel to be discharged. Although the thunderous detonation of the ten-gauge firing charge momentarily reduced her ability to hear, she was not so deafened that she could not hear the scream of a man in agony and what followed.

"There's a *man* in here!" bellowed a voice, and the clatter of a can being dropped followed immediately.

Knowing what had brought the intruders to the ranch house, Margaret did not hesitate in the slightest. She turned the shotgun and fired again, controlling the powerful recoil kick in a way that was indicative of the wiry strength she possessed. Once more, a pain-filled vocal response gave proof that her aim was good. However, she also heard the footsteps of another man running toward the house, and she knew the danger to her was far from over. There was an open box of shells for her weapon on the table, and because she had often practiced the maneuver, she knew she could locate the table and carry out the reloading process. However, the time to do so was not granted to her.

Even as Margaret was breaking open the shotgun's action to eject the spent cases, there was a diversion which she badly needed. Letting out a roaring snarl, the big retriever hurled himself from his sitting position and through the window. Alighting outside, he charged forward and again launched himself into the air. Struck by eighty pounds of attacking dog, the man who had posed the latest threat to Margaret was knocked over backward. Winded by his descent to the ground, he was unable to prevent the dog's powerful jaws from sinking teeth into his throat. As he struggled ineffectually to escape the choking pressure, there were other disruptions of the scheme that had brought him and five companions to the Wedge's ranch house.

Clad in a most becoming nightgown, with her blond hair disheveled, April came running into Margaret's room holding the Colt Storekeeper Peacemaker she kept on her bedside table. Also carrying weapons, Peaceful Gunn—who had returned from delivering the body of Dusty Fog's attacker shortly before the women retired—and the other men who had been left as guards came from the bunkhouse. A moment later, armed with a shotgun, Jose Martinez dashed out of the house in which he and his wife made their home.

None of the ranch crew's members had any means of illumination with them. However, after what had happened to the pair making for the main house to carry out the arson there, the appearance of the armed men was enough to prompt the surviving intruders to call it quits and escape. There were a few shots fired on both sides, but none hit their mark. Then, having discarded the cans of kerosene, the intruders headed at a run for their horses and rode away swiftly. Having only been struck by two of the nine buckshot balls from the second barrel of Margaret's shotgun—neither striking a vital area—the second man to receive her attentions joined in the flight.

Peaceful assumed command of the ranch's men. Knowing his ability as a fighter, the others raised no objections. They all collected lanterns from the bunkhouse, having decided it was safe for them to do so when the intruders gave no indication of returning. With the illumination the lanterns provided, they discovered that the first man shot by their boss lady was dead. Furthermore, although they had to wait until Margaret came out of the ranch house, guided by April, and called to Rollo to leave off the attack, they found there was nothing to fear from the intruder who had fallen victim to the dog.

"Best go inside 'n' leave things to us, ladies," Peaceful requested. "They're not like' to be coming back, but we'll keep a damned careful watch in case they do."

12
I WISH I'D LIVED
A BETTER 'N' CLEANER LIFE

"May I be 'ternally damned for saying it," Calamity Jane declared with seeming truculence and even a suggestion of shame. However, her voice betrayed the genuine feeling behind the words. "But I'm real sorry that I've got to leave off taking care of you fellers. Trouble being, Dobe here allows he just can't get along without my invaluable services."

"That's *unvaluable*," corrected Cecil "Dobe" Killem as he eyed in mock derision the redheaded girl whom he had accepted as a member of his freight-wagon outfit and had helped train to be a most competent driver. "I don't suppose you'd be willing to keep her on, now would you, Dusty?"

"I'd be honored to oblige you, sir," the small Texan said, and contrived to sound disappointed. Only, things've been sort of quiet and peaceful around here the last few days. Why, we haven't even had us some gals—two who should've known better—getting into a hair-yanking, kicking, hitting, 'n' biting knock-down, dragout brawl of late. Fact being, things've been so quiet, the city fathers're starting to reckon they're paying out good money to keep so many of us in sloth idleness."

"Then it looks like *I'm* stuck with her!" Killem groaned. "Times I wish I'd lived a better 'n' cleaner life."

"You'd've been hard pushed to do that with *her* around," Rusty Willis asserted. "She even led my sweet, innocent, meek 'n' mild li'l wife astray with her wicked ways."

"Now, me," Thorny Bush put in, ready to take whatever action should become necessary to avoid the retaliation he expected from Calamity. "I allus thought her 'n' your sweet, innocent, meek 'n' mild li'l wife needed no leading. Fact being, I concluded they was twin sisters, way they talk 'n' act."

"To hell with the whole boiling of you!" the redhead spat out. "Don't ask me why I should, 'specially when I'm cold sober, but I love every last blasted useless one of you. Only, you tell Steffie that's in a *brotherly* way where you're concerned, Rusty, seeing as she's one gal I don't want to tangle with unless she's siding me. Let's be going, Dobe, afore we all break into sniveling."

Five days had elapsed since the rear of the jailhouse was blown up and the occupants of the cells killed. During that time, there had been only a few positive developments, and none of these were on the matter to which Dusty Fog and his deputies had devoted so much of their attention. That Robin C. Harman was shot to death after having survived the explosion had struck him as significant. It seemed likely that the one responsible either knew or believed the banker possessed incriminating knowledge and was determined that it would not be given to anybody. That Calamity could have also been badly hurt, or killed, had given all three of the Texans an extra inducement to solve the mystery. However, when they questioned the people who had assembled, they had failed to find anyone who had seen the explosives being put against the wall or even a person in the vicinity of the building.

On the morning after the incident, there had been an unexpected development. Clad in clothing suitable for appearing in public and having unsuccessfully tried to conceal their facial injuries, the female employees of the cantina had come to the jailhouse, where Steffie Willis was about to leave for the Wedge ranch house. Acting as their spokeswoman, Winnie Ashwell had apologized for having caused the fight and claimed Calamity had whipped her younger sister—who, she said, had probably asked for everything that was done—fair and square. She had also thanked the ash-blonde for the consideration shown in ensuring that none of them had sustained serious injury. Having stated that there were no hard feeling, and supported in this by Steffie, the redhead had said that "anytime you gals want another round, don't call *us*, we'll call you." On that cheerful note of conciliation, the visit was brought to an amiable end.

Derek Hatton and Steven Scott had requested and been granted permission by Calamity and Steffie to name their establishment the Battling Belles Saloon. Already the myth had started that the fight had taken place on the premises instead of in the woodland beyond the town's limits. Eventually, a painting of what was supposed to have taken place was commissioned and placed on the wall behind the bar in the main room, although none of the actual participants were identifiable in the portrait and the loss of attire was not depicted fully. Furthermore, with the passing of time, the event achieved a fame similar to that accorded an earlier multicombatant female fight that took place in Bearcat Annie's saloon at Quiet Town.[1]

After the women had returned to their living quarters and Rusty had seen his wife head back to the Wedge, Dusty put all his deputies to the task of seeing what could be learned about the explosion. Accompanied by Calamity, he visited all the houses in the neighborhood in the hope that somebody who had not been outside the jailhouse the previous night had seen something of help. This had proved fruitless, as had investigations by the other two Texans.

Having returned from his fishing trip to resume his duties as jailer, Liam Fox had cursed himself for being away when Sheriff Amon Reeves was shot. Then he had put his considerable knowledge of prospecting to use examining the damage to the back of the jailhouse, and had stated that it could only have been caused by dynamite or nitroglycerine. Sent to try to find out where such potent explosives had been obtained, Rusty and Bush interviewed the owner of Clitheroe's

1. What caused the "fight at Bearcat Annie's," as the conflict had already become known, is told in QUIET TOWN.
   1a. *We do not know why there was no depiction of the fight on the outskirts of Child City in the collection of paintings purporting to illustrate other female fracases in the Old West, to which we refer in* RAPIDO CLINT.

General Emporium and the proprietor of the local gunsmith's, the most likely sources. Both had said that no one had purchased any explosives.

Asked by the two Texans, William Morris had said that it was the policy of Wells Fargo to warn agents along the route when potentially dangerous commodities were being transported on one of their stagecoaches and that he had received no such notification. Dobe Killem followed the same rule for shipments carried on his freight wagons, and Calamity had said there was no mention of explosives on the manifest for the consignment she had helped deliver to the cantina. However, she had pointed out that she believed Hatton and Scott were sneaky enough to have concealed explosives in boxes supposed to contain legitimate items for use in their business. Dusty pointed out that they were smart enough to have disposed of any remaining dynamite, if indeed they were guilty of the crime, and had declined her suggestion that a search be made of their premises.

The arrival later in the day of news sent by Mark Counter about what had happened the previous night at the Wedge ranch house had only added to the small Texan's problems. Neither of the men killed the previous night had anything on their persons or saddles to identify them. Nor were they carrying large sums of money like those found on the pair of hired guns. Therefore, Dusty had surmised that they had a hiding place to which they could return instead of taking flight if things went wrong.

Unfortunately, as was the case with the abortive attempt to ambush his big blond *amigo,* the small Texan could think of no one with the skill to read tracks well enough to follow the survivors of the thwarted arson attempt. Therefore, he had passed word back for the guards at all the ranches to be extra vigilant during nighttime hours, and he knew the same would be told to the cowhands working the roundup. He had hated to have to take such a passive approach, but in light of recent events, he had reluctantly accepted that he had his duty to do as town marshal of Child City rather than sheriff for Spanish Grant County.

About three hours after the instructions were dispatched, there was a solution to one part of the problem. Sitting his massive white stallion, which was leg-weary from having traveled from Prescott in the fashion learned during his training as a member of the Pehnane Comanche Dog Soldier war lodge, the Ysabel Kid arrived in Child City. Told what had happened, he had said he would be ready to head out to join Mark after both he and Nigger were rested. Dusty had hoped that the Kid's presence would not be noticed so he could conduct his specialized inquiries on the range unsuspected. However, somebody had clearly recognized him, and word of his coming had spread all around the town before nightfall. The following morning, although a heavy rain shower had washed away all the tracks at the Wedge ranch house, the Kid had started to search for the origins of the men responsible for the attempted arson.

For the next four days, everything had remained peaceful throughout the whole of Spanish Grant Country.

The Kid had sent word to Dusty on the second day of scouting the range that a long-disused adobe line cabin on the outer fringes of the Arrow P, along the border of Spanish Grant County, showed signs of recent occupancy by an indeterminate number of men. However, they had left shortly after the ground had dried out, and what tracks were discernible showed they had crossed the county line. They had chosen terrain over which the reading of tracks was extremely difficult, and after following the tracks for a few miles with no sign of their turning back, he had decided to return. Either the Kid's reputation as a deadly efficient adversary had decided the hired guns against further depredations, or they had been ordered to desist for some other reason. In any event, there was no further trouble on the range and the roundup continued successfully.

Dusty and his deputies passed the time in the usual routine of a Western town. The crews of the four ranches remained fully occupied with the roundup or keeping watch on the ranches, so they were only rarely present in town. In fact, apart from a couple of fistfights and the occasional rowdy drunk, Bush found little to keep him busy.

One possible problem had not arisen. When the Arizona State Saloon reopened, the cantina, with renovations still far from complete and many of supplies still needed, had still stayed in business. However, it was soon obvious to Dusty that, as yet at least, there was no need to compete for trade, since Angus McTavish had built up a steady clientele among the older citizens and others.

The cantina had become the place where the hired guns gravitated. Bush commented that this struck him as suspicious, but Calamity pointed out that men like them tended to seek out places where the influential members of the community did not go. Dusty agreed, stating that there would be no difference in the way the two saloons were treated unless something happened at the newer establishment to make a change of the policy necessary.

Called in as a matter of legal procedure by Counselor Edward Sutherland in his capacity as justice of the peace for Spanish Grant County, an official bank examiner had arrived from Prescott to conduct an investigation into the evidence of malpractice revealed by Amos Clitheroe. Far more experienced in such matters than the storekeeper, the examiner concluded that Harman was merely a figurehead and that the establishment was owned by a person or persons unknown.

Dusty had already suspected this, and he concluded that Harman had known from whom the formidable Mrs. Harriet Harman had obtained the position for him and was withholding the information in an attempt to save himself. Such a supposition would explain why he was killed. Clearly somebody had wanted to take no chances of Harman's being frightened into telling what he knew.

The small Texan had continued to give thought to who in Child City might be behind the trouble that had continued after the death of Eustace Edgar Eisteddfod. He had felt that some recent arrivals were possible suspects: William Morris at the Wells Fargo office, James

Knapp, who had taken over the livery barn on the retirement of the previous owner, Counselor Nigel Jones, and the two men who operated the cantina. Morris had access to all incoming and outgoing telegraph messages, which could account for the attempted ambush of Stone Hart and Major Wilson Eardle. And because the majority of the hired guns used Knapp's facilities for stabling their horses, they would be able to leave town to carry out assignments without their departure being known to anybody except him. However, as far as Dusty had been able to tell, all of these suspects were leading blameless lives. Therefore, he had been compelled to cast his net wider.

Not having heard that Jack Straw had left Prescott, the Kid had failed to mention to Dusty his suspicions after Straw was pointed out by Kiowa Cotton. Therefore, Straw's arrival in Child City two days after the black-dressed Texan went on the scouting assignment had aroused no more than passing interest. Straw was experienced enough to know that his presence had been noticed by the local peace officers, and when they met at the Arizona State Saloon, he had told Rusty and the youngster that he was resting before riding on to his next employment. Dusty had concluded that Straw was better quality than any of the other hired guns hanging around the town, and that he had done nothing to warrant further curiosity. Therefore, Straw was left largely to his own devices. Unbeknownst to the small Texan and the temporary members of the sheriff's office, his time was being spent trying to discover who had been hiring and sending other gunfighters to Spanish Grant County.

The arrival of Dobe Killem with the remainder of the stores and equipment for the newly named Battling Belles Saloon had ended the reason for Calamity to stay on in the town. Although she had offered to stay and her boss said he did not object, Dusty said there was no longer any need for her services. Nobody expressed the sentiment in words, but they would be sorry to see the feisty redhead depart.

"Well, that's her gone and more work for us two, Rusty," Bush commented after Calamity had given a kiss and a hug all around to the three Texans, including a stamp on his toe and a warning to watch his manners when ladies were around. "Things'll sure be quieter around here without her."

"Which I'm all for a quiet life," Dusty declared, then eyed the two remaining deputies. "I could be wrong, but I've got just the teensiest sneaking suspicion that the good taxpaying folks of Spanish Grant County expect more from their deputy sheriffs than just standing 'round moping 'cause that red-topped lump of perversity's left."

"Do you reckon we're being told something, Deputy Sheriff Willis?" the youngster inquired, looking quizzical.

"That I do, Deputy Sheriff Bush," Rusty declared, nodding as if supplying sage advice. "So what say we go and make out like we're earning all that money the good taxpaying folks of Spanish Grant County hand over for our invaluable services."

"Dobe was right," the small Texan growled. *"Unvaluable* is the word."

13
THE NAME'S CHARLIE HENRY

"Hello, Myrtle," April Eardle greeted.

"Holy Mother of God!" the slender grizzled-brunette saloon girl who was currently calling herself Fifi le Planchet gasped, staring in alarm, then amazement and relief. Her accent became noticeably less French as recognition came and she continued, "Why, 'tis you yourself, Miss Hosman."

April had received a message from Mrs. Flora McTavish asking her to pay a visit to the members of the Child City Civic Betterment League to discuss the show in aid of obtaining a new roof for the schoolhouse she was helping to organize, and she had had a second reason for deciding to accept. She had learned of the fight on the return of Steffie Willis to the Wedge ranch house and found the reference to the willowy woman with the French name of interest.

Having satisfied herself that the ash-blonde was capable of keeping the tally book while she was gone—and giving a humorous warning that she did not want her dear boys taught any bad language by her deputy in her absence—April had left to change into more suitable attire for the meeting. She was relieved to be able to wear feminine attire, although she had enjoyed being in male garb when at the bunch ground. While donning a stylish dress

142

obtained from Selina of Polveroso, Texas, that was figure-flattering without the risk of drawing disapproval from the women she was going to meet, she had decided not to go into town alone.[1] But this decision was not out of concern for her safety on the journey. She had felt Margaret Hart needed to get away from the Wedge ranch house for a short while as an aid to forgetting the attempted arson and her role in it.

She had left Margaret at the Sutherland family's home, then, having learned where the women employed by the Battling Belles Saloon were accommodated, had gone there ostensibly to collect the items of their working clothes that Steffie had requested were loaned. Good fortune had favored her, and the one she was seeking was just coming out as she arrived. Before she had married Major Wilson Eardle, the blonde had saved Fifi le Planchet—who at the time was using the name Myrtle Muldoon—from arrest when she had become the innocent dupe of a bunch of confidence tricksters. She had often declared that she would do anything she could to return the favor. Although she did not know it, the time had come for her to be put to the test.

"Not Hosman anymore, Fifi," April corrected with a smile. "I've been saved from a life of sin and am now a respectable married woman. Anyway, I hear that you and the other girls at the old cantina got yourselves into a fuss with two friends of mine."

1. The significance of a dress from Selina of Polveroso, Texas, is explained in TEXAS KIDNAPPERS.

"That we did, Miss April, and I'll not be denying it to you," the grizzled brunette said with a wry grin, unable to revert to her French accent in the presence of the person she revered above anybody else she had ever known. She gestured to her face, where the heavy make-up she had applied could not conceal the marks left by the conflict. "And you being friends with 'em, it's knowing you'll be that it was a sound drubbing we got for our pains."

"You gave some of it back," the blonde reminded, thinking about how Steffie had looked after the fight. Her glance flickered to where a rider was passing and threw a quick look her way without giving any sign of recognition to suggest he was an acquaintance from her single days. Returning her attention almost immediately to the slender woman, she went on, "And you can go back to your French accent. How do you like working hereabouts?"

"It beats being somewhere that Wyatt Earp's taking a cut from," Fifi asserted, reverting to her accent as was suggested. "But not by much."

"Did Winnie Ashwell really have a sister Calamity Jane beat in a fight?"

"I'd never heard of it. She just said the bosses had told her to have Calam beat up because of what happened to their dog. Although she reckoned she could do it herself, we got told to go along to help her if she needed it. Well, she soon looked like she needed it and, being her, li'l Doxie—who I don't reckon you know—well, she just *had* to go to give it."

"That's just about what I figured," April

admitted. She refrained from mentioning that she had been told the grizzled-brunette was also a leader in joining in the fray. "Who are Hatton and Scott and where are they from? They're new to me, but let's not forget I haven't been around for a spell."

"They're new to me, and I have," the grizzled-brunette admitted. "I was looking for somewhere new to work over to Santa Fe and heard they were hiring in Albuquerque, only I don't think they had a place there. At least they, nor nobody else, mentioned them having or moving out of one when I saw them and got took on."

"Would you say they're big bosses, or just running things for somebody else?"

"Nothing's been said, but I've got the feeling they're only hired help like the rest of us, 'cept they get better paid and don't work so hard."

"Do you know if they've got somebody higher up keeping watch on them here?"

"I've never heard either of 'em mention it out loud," Fifi answered, wondering what the conversation was leading up to, since she felt sure the blonde was not merely making idle talk. "But I've a notion that they could have. Only, they're not the kind you show nosy over. Not twice, anyways."

"Mean, are they?"

"I've knowed a lot who were gentler 'n' only a few who're worse," Fifi said grimly. "Did you come to see me about something special, Miss—Miz April?"

"I did," the blonde admitted. "But I've changed my mind—!"

"What's up, Miss April?" the grizzled-brunette asked as the words died away. She turned her head in the direction the blonde was looking, where another horseman was passing with no more than a glance toward them on the far side of the street. "Does he know you?"

"He may have seen me around someplace in the old days, but I'd say it's *you* he was interested in," the blonde replied. "Anyway, I've just changed my mind again. There *is* something I want you to do, but it could be risky as hell."

"I'll take my chance on *that!*" Fifi stated, satisfied with the explanation despite wondering what had caused the change in April's intentions. "When you saved me from going to jail for as long as it would have been, I told you that you'd only got to ask me to do *anything* for you and it'd be done."

"Very well, but I don't want you to run any risks. Have you heard about all the trouble that's been happening around here lately?"

"You mean that bunch wanting to lynch them two fellers who they reckon robbed the bank and killed the young feller who worked there?"

"That and more," April replied, and gave a couple of examples.

"Do you reckon Hatton 'n' Scott are mixed up in it?"

"There's a chance they could be. So I'd like you to keep your eyes and ears open for anything that doesn't set right with you and, even more important, if you see anybody around who could be their boss."

146

"I can do that easy enough," Fifi claimed without hesitation. "How do I let you know anything I find out?"

"Something tells me there'll be a couple of fellers around the cantina who'll be only too willing to pass the word," April replied. Then she gave certain instructions for the grizzled-brunette to follow if there was news. With that done, and after being assured she was understood, April concluded, "And now I'd better be getting on with the other thing I've come here for."

★   ★   ★

"Howdy, mister," said the only bartender on duty at the Battling Belles Saloon, running a knowing gaze over the customer who had just arrived at the counter. The time was just before sundown and business was still slack. "You're new around here."

"I'm new," the man replied in a lazy Texas drawl that nevertheless was pitched hard and unfriendly. "'N' I don't take kind' to folks being nosy. Pour me a big cold beer 'n' take one for yourself."

Although he had not cared for being addressed in such a manner, the bulky, muscular man behind the counter did as he was instructed without objection. There was something about the newcomer that suggested the bartender was wise not to have pressed the issue. Wearing the attire of a working cowhand that showed only signs of recent travel, the newcomer was about six feet tall and sturdily built without being bulky. The shoved-back

147

brown J. B. Stetson hat, its low crown indicative of origins in Texas, revealed untidy and fiery red hair. Ruggedly good-looking, his whisker-stubbled face was set in hard lines. About his waist was a well-designed gunbelt with the butts of two walnut-handled Colt Cavalry Model Peacemakers turned forward for a low twist-hand draw well suited for their long barrels. Having noticed the wolf-cautious way in which he scanned the barroom before entering, the counterman concluded that the newcomer was a competent gunfighter and was probably always hired by somebody who needed skill with a gun.

"Gracias," the Texan drawled in a more amiable tone, accepting the large schooner of beer he was given with the satisfaction of one who had been waiting for the chance to do so for some time. "I hear tell there's some riding chores going around these parts?"

"Sure," the bartender replied. He noticed he had been paid from a wad of ten-dollar bills and that there was no rush to pick up the change. "There's a roundup for all the spreads in the county going on."

"And it can keep going, for all of me," the redhead claimed, having drunk half the beer while the answer was being given. "Mrs. Henry didn't raise her sweet 'n' loving li'l ole boy Charlie to work no goddamned roundup."

"I haven't heard tell of nothing else being wanted," the bartender declared truthfully. "Though I'll admit there's been a few of you hire—fellers who don't take kind' to working on roundup been drifting in and out just recent."

"Wonder if there's anybody I know among 'em?" the man who called himself Charles Henry remarked in an offhand fashion.

"Ain't nobody real special," the bartender answered, deciding that the name was a summer name rather than one given at birth. "Not less'n you count Jack Straw that high."

"Can't say as how I've ever heard tell of him," Henry admitted, still without showing any interest. Turning to lean against the counter, he again looked around the room. However, he now seemed to be devoting more of his attention to the female occupants than the few other customers who were present. "Air these ladies some of the battling belles as are meant by your sign?"

"The very same," the bartender confirmed. "They took on Calamity Jane 'n' a whole bunch of her shemale friends 'n' whupped 'em to a frazzle."

"Now, I bet *that* was a sight to see," the redhead declared. "Did *you* see it?"

"Well, no," the bartender denied. "I wasn't working that afternoon, blast it."

"That's allus the way," Henry said, but without any noticeable commiseration. His attention was focused on Fifi le Planchet, who was approaching. Removing his hat with his right hand, he greeted, "Why, howdy, ma'am. From the looks of you, I'd be willing to bet that it was *you* who did most of the whupping on Calamity Jane 'n' her bunch."

The grizzled-brunette had left a table where she and Doxie Rimmer had reluctantly been in the company of two of the local loafers. Like her friend, she knew them to be the kind who thought that paying for a beer—while drinking the cheapest whiskey offered by the place and not holding it well—allowed them to take liberties with women such as pawing and manhandling. Nor did they ever go higher than a single beer, since they rarely had much money. Chance rather than a desire for better company had caused her to go toward where the red-haired newcomer was standing. She had merely intended to ask the bartender to warn the pair at her table to improve their behavior. However, the way she was addressed by the newcomer told her she would be better off staying where she was.

"I did my share of it, m'sieur," Fifi said. She had no intention of correcting the misapprehension over who was involved in—or the result of—the fight.

"I bet not even April Hosman in her day could've done better," the Texan asserted loudly. "The name's Charlie Henry from Waxahachie, Texas, ma'am. Would you do me the *honor* of taking something?" Seeing the way in which the grizzled-brunette glanced at the half-filled schooner that his left hand grasped by its stem, he went on, "Shucks, I wouldn't ask a for-real French lady like you to take nothing but wine, ma'am."

"Well, I am with my friend—!" Fifi began, knowing Doxie would not care to be left alone in the company of the loafers—Arthur Lawrence and George Martin by name—even if they had not reached such a stage of obnoxious behavior.

"Then call her over to join you, ma'am," Henry suggested, still speaking in a louder voice than was necessary. "Like I said, no lady should have to drink beer."

"You stay put, Doxie!" Lawrence commanded as the little buxom blonde began to rise. Clad in untidy and unclean town-dweller and range clothes, he was the slightly taller and heavier of the pair. His manner of speech clearly showed he was feeling the effects of the small amount of liquor he had consumed. "And you can haul your ass back here right now, Frenchie!"

"Get the lady her wine, mister," Henry ordered, directing the words over his shoulder and laying his Stetson on the bar. "And one for her friend, comes to that."

"Come on, Art!" Martin snarled, his voice slurred as Doxie rose and made for the bar. "Let's hand that beefhead bastard his needings."

"Let's do just that, George," Lawrence agreed. He was also a troublemaker when he had had even a few drinks.

Looking over his shoulder as he was reaching for a bottle of wine, the bartender let out a low growl of annoyance. However, before he could do anything more, the matter was taken from his hands in no uncertain fashion. Thrusting himself erect and advancing toward them, Henry flung the contents of the schooner into Martin's face and slammed its solid base against the side of the other loafer's jaw. The force of the impact sent Lawrence spinning to the floor. Before Martin could clear his vision, the Texan had pivoted his way and swung the schooner at the side of his head. Martin sprawled stunned on the unyielding hard-packed adobe surface of the saloon.

Such was the speed of the attack that the bartender was unable to keep up with it. He had been moving closer to the counter with the intention of siding with Henry. However, unaware of his good intentions and knowing saloon workers tended to side with patrons they knew over strangers, Henry was ready to deal with whatever action the bartender might be contemplating.

Turning his right hand palm outward, the red-haired Texan closed his hand around the walnut butt of the off-side Colt and, in a twisting motion that served to let his thumb cock the hammer, brought it from its holster. While made at only about half the speed a tophand *pistolero* could produce, the draw was sufficiently swift for his needs. Directed by instinctive alignment, the seven-and-a-half-inch barrel halted when it was pointing at the bartender's face. Under the circumstances, the man behind the counter thought the muzzle to be far larger than its .45-caliber bore, and the threat it posed brought him to an immediate halt, alarm showing on his face.

"You conclude on taking it up for 'em?" Henry demanded.

"He *doesn't!*" Derek Hatton asserted in a loud voice with a New England accent, as a similar assurance was given by the bartender. Hatton had watched all that happened with some interest and walked forward. "So you can put the gun up, friend."

"You the boss here?" the Texan inquired without doing as was requested.

"One of them," Hatton replied. "Have those two bums throwed out of here, some of you. And you can let our friend from Texas have him his next order on the house, Tom."

152

"*All* of it?" Henry queried with a grin, twirling away the Colt.

"Well, I'll admit we'd likely draw the line at half of our stock," the New Englander answered. "What have you in mind?"

"A bottle of wine for the French lady here 'n' some for her beautiful li'l *amigo,* for starters," the Texan drawled, slipping an arm around the grizzled-brunette's slender waist in a proprietary fashion. "Then for her to be let come show me the sights of the town, which I'd surely like to see—'specially like where she lives."

"That all right with you, Fifi?" Hatton asked, but his tone was more declarative than questioning. He had made an arrangement with the owner of the small boardinghouse where the saloon girls rented rooms whereby they would be permitted to take male visitors there.

"I have no objections, M'sieur Hatton," the grizzled-brunette claimed. "In fact, I think it will be the fun to show Charlie Henry the *sights.*"

"Who is he?" the New Englander demanded of the bartender after Fifi and the redhead had left the room.

"Allows he's Charlie Henry, like the Froggie said," the burly man replied, having accepted that the grizzled-brunette was indeed of French extraction. "And allows he hails from someplace in Texas. I can't say as how I've ever heard of him, only I wasn't figuring on letting him know *that.*"

"Then he could be using what you out here call a summer name?" Hatton suggested.

"Could be, 'n' more'n likely is," the bartender replied. "Only, I didn't figure on asking if it be, 'n' way that gun came out, I'm right pleased I didn't."

"Did he say what he was doing here?" the New Englander queried.

"Looking for work, and he made it plain he don't mean just riding the range chasing cattle," the barman answered.

"Then maybe some can be found for him that don't call for it when he gets back from seeing the sights," Hatton stated. "I'll see him when he does, and I hope it'll be afore morning."

14
MARVIN ELDRIDGE, FROM AMARILLO, TEXAS

The man who came into the barroom of the Battling Belles Saloon at half past eight in the evening had on the attire of a professional gambler. About six feet tall and slimly built, yet exuding a sense of hidden power, he had black hair and a neatly trimmed mustache. Not unexpectedly, in view of the way he was dressed, his good-looking features had a pallor that suggested he did not spend much of the daylight hours in the open air. Nevertheless, he moved with a light-footed stride and his hands seemed almost boneless.

His appearance said that the newcomer was in a lucky streak. With the exception of his well-polished black boots, which had the high heels and sharp toes more commonly seen on the footwear of cowhands, his clothes looked to be new. He had on a white planter's hat with a wide brim and low crown, a black cutaway jacket, a frilly-bosomed white shirt whose neck was closed with a black string bow tie, and tight-legged gray trousers with a black stripe down the outer seam. The right side of the coat had been stitched back to allow unimpeded access to the ivory-handled Colt Civilian Model Peacemaker revolver in the contoured holster of a gunbelt, which was clearly of excellent manufacture.

Having scanned his surroundings with a casual gaze, then waved aside the saloon girls who came toward him with a polite gesture of his left hand, the newcomer strolled around, looking at each gambling game as he went. Derek Hatton and Steven Scott, who watched him covertly, had mixed emotions when he went back to a table where a five-handed game of stud poker was taking place. He asked if he could sit in and was given an answer in the affirmative. Then he reached for the nearest unoccupied chair, placed it between two of the players, hung his hat by its fancy-plaited leather barbiquejo chin strap on the chair's back, and sat down.

Knowing the game to be for the highest stakes in the room, since three of the players were hired guns with a lot of money to wager, it struck the New Englander—whose specialty was the business side of the saloon's activities—as the most suitable for their purposes. One of saloon employers was acting as cutter—in fact, he went by the name Cutter—and served as supervisor for the house. In addition to setting the rules for the benefit of

155

new players and serving as arbitrator in all matters, he deducted a percentage of each pot to cover expenses. Although he did not play, or even handle the cards himself, two other men at the table who were employed by the saloon did. To prevent the connection from being suspected, they had been introduced as a traveling salesman and a lucky mining prospector. Furthermore, the New Englander and his partner had decided that the precepts that would be explained should the gambler join the game would place the newcomer—like the three other players not employed by the saloon—at a great disadvantage.

Still, Scott had misgivings. The game being played, five card high-low stud, seemingly increased each player's chances of taking, or at least sharing equally in, a pot on a showdown by making it possible for him to decide whether the hand he was dealt was of sufficient strength to win or so low in rank that nobody else in the pot could hold one of lesser value. The one holding the best hand—having already announced he was going for "high"—and another declaring for "low" would divide the money wagered evenly between them. The variation in the current rules was that the player who was being called for a showdown had to expose his hole card to let the value of his hand be seen. By doing so, he allowed the other players who had not withdrawn from the betting to decide in which direction they wished their cards to be valued.

"Feel free, friend," Cutter had said when asked by the newcomer for permission to join the game. Short, stocky, yet sharp-featured,

Cutter wore the garb of a gambler, although he frequently claimed truthfully that he had never made a bet in his life and never intended to. He was content to be in a supervisory capacity, he said, and had the skill to detect cheating. Expecting an answer in the negative taking into account how the other was dressed, he continued, "It's no-limit, five-card high-low with no wild cards. The one called has to say which he's holding and show. Is that all right with you?"

"Why, surely so, sir and gentlemen," the slender gambler had replied, his voice indicative of origins in Texas. "Choosing high or low gives a man *two* chances of winning every pot."

"Name's Cutter," the houseman introduced after the newcomer had sat down. He was puzzled by the immediate acceptance of the rules, and concluded that the newcomer had less knowledge of gambling than was suggested by his clothing. Deciding that this could prove beneficial for the other two saloon workers, he indicated the players in turn. "This is Beale, Denton, Glasser—he says he travels in ladies unmentionables, only not wearing 'em, to save the rest of us having to hear it again—Tarry, and Hard-Rock. I'd best warn you about Hard-Rock—he's struck lucky with a gold claim and it's rubbed off on his playing the way he's winning."

"You can say *that* again," the florid-faced and loudly dressed Glasser growled. "All the luck's going *his* way."

"Not *all* of it," Cutter corrected, as he was required to do to suggest that no collusion was taking place between the pair. Hard-Rock looked like a less-than-clean elderly desert-rat prospector despite the fact that he had struck it rich recently. "*Everybody's* had their share of the pots."

"Gentlemen," the newcomer drawled, acknowledging each name with an inclination of his head. The place he had selected—he claimed it was his lucky position—put him across the table from Glasser and Hard-Rock. Knowing that even professional gamblers were inclined toward such superstitions, no one objected to the choice, although Cutter remarked in a light fashion that the other players might be ill-advised to let him sit somewhere likely to improve his luck. "The name's Marvin Eldridge, from Amarillo, Texas."

With the formalities concluded, the game was resumed. Watching everything that happened with keen and knowing eyes, Cutter soon concluded that Eldridge knew less about gambling than was at first suspected. The houseman decided that Eldridge must have only recently taken up the occupation and was not overproficient at it. Going by the pallor of his features, although he appeared fit enough otherwise, he could be suffering from consumption—as pulmonary tuberculosis was called—and had chosen such a way of earning a living as more active occupations were barred from him.

One thing was for sure, Cutter decided: If the amount of money Eldridge had placed on the table was any guide, he was far from being close to the blanket. The houseman wondered whether the newcomer's gun and belt had been purchased to give the impression that he was tougher and more competent than he in fact was. When asked to cut the deck—a courtesy extended to every new player—he said, "Cut 'em light, lose all night" and he won two out of the first three pots. When his turn to deal came around, he gave the deck a perfunctory overhand stack rather than the professional's thorough riffling.

Satisfied that the newcomer would pose no threat to the way the game was being run, Cutter watched, amused, the smooth way in which Glasser and Hard-Rock carried out their part in ensuring that the house turned a profit. Neither possessed ability in the more subtle forms of cheating, such as stacking the deck or dealing the second instead of the top card. However, they each had the skill to palm and hold back a card of high rank, then substitute it when required to strengthen a hand. Different positions indicated the value of the hole card for the benefit of the other partner. In addition, they were adept at sandbagging without making the technique obvious: With Glasser complaining that he felt an attempt was being made to force him out, each man continued to bet and raise until a player, possibly holding a stronger hand than either of theirs, dropped out of the betting.

From the beginning, Cutter had noticed that none of the hired guns had made the most of their opportunities. Furthermore, Eldridge had given little indication of being better informed. Therefore, the team working for the house were already the major winners in the game. However, by a combination of good—

or bad—hands and what could only be lucky estimation of whether to go for "high" or "low," considering the unskillful way he played at other times, the pallid-faced Texan ran them a close second.

The deal came round to Hard-Rock. Eldridge received a king in the hole, and his next card was the same denomination. With the ace of clubs as his first displayed card, Glasser changed the hole card for the ace of hearts, which he had palmed earlier. He had made the move so deftly that even Cutter failed to detect the switch. For once, none of the hired guns had cards they considered worth playing, and they folded. However, the Texan continued to bet and raise in his usual reckless fashion and gave no indication of realizing that he could not have better than the pair when the last cards were dealt. Against that, neither of his opponents had even that much showing. From the comments made by the Texan as the betting progressed, the stocky houseman assumed that he believed the other two were staying in only to oppose one another for low hand. Their actual intention, Cutter knew, was to put Eldridge between them so Glasser won high and Hard-Rock low, allowing them to share the pot.

"Call," Glasser said, judging that the Texan intended to do so and wanting to put the onus of selection on him.

"High on a pair of kings," Eldridge accepted, turning over his hole card.

"Low on ten high to nothing," Hard-Rock announced, and proved he did not have any kind of a pair.

"*High* on two little bullets!" Glasser declared with a smug grin. "It looks like you run second both ways twixt 'n' between me 'n' Hard-Rock, Amarillo."

"Why, sure," Eldridge answered in a mild fashion. "Except you switched in that ace from the hole, so let's see what's tucked down there under your rump."

While speaking, the Texan had thrust his chair skidding from beneath him and come to his feet. Also rising, although not with quite the same alacrity, Glasser sent his right hand across to where he was carrying a short-barreled Colt Storekeeper Model Peacemaker tucked into his waistband. He and his partner had needed to deal with similar situations in the past, and they had developed a technique that had never failed them. It was his intention to hold the Texan's attention and allow Hard-Rock to cut in unexpectedly should this be needed.

Hard-Rock quickly concluded that he would be required to play his part, even though doing so might arouse suspicions about his relationship with the supposed salesman.

There was a white flicker as Eldridge commenced a draw. So swiftly did the ivory-handled Colt leave its well-designed holster, it almost seemed to the onlookers to meet his descending hand in midair. In addition, he showed a remarkably good grasp of the situation. Instead of concentrating solely on Glasser, he saw that the Colt 1860 Army revolver—which had been rechambered to take metallic cartridges as part of Hard-Rock's pose as an elderly desert-rat prospector—was being drawn.

Instead of turning the Peacemaker into alignment on Glasser, the Texan swung it and sent a bullet into the other partner's shoulder.

Even as Hard-Rock was spinning around and going down with a cry of pain—and allowing his weapon to fall from fingers that had suddenly lost all power to hold on—Eldridge dealt with the other menace. Cocking the Colt on its recoil, he sent his second shot into the right side of Glasser's chest. The speed with which the change of direction was made allowed this to happen before Glasser's weapon could be brought around and used. He reeled backward and measured his length on the floor as the gun left his hand. The Texan once again cocked his Colt and swung a rapid gaze around him that settled for a moment on Cutter, who spread his hands with the palms open and outward away from his sides to establish beyond any doubt his pacific intentions.

"There's a card under that so-called drummer's chair, friend," Eldridge stated. "Pick it up and show everybody in the room."

"Do you know him?" Derek Hatton asked a hired gun to whom he had been talking by the bar.

"Nope," the man replied. "But I *should,* way he handles that Colt."

"Would you say he's as fast as Dusty Fog?" the New Englander inquired in a speculative fashion.

"I'd hate to have my life hang on the difference," the hired gun admitted, then nodded toward the batwing doors. "Could be you'll have a chance to find out!"

Looking in the same direction, Hatton saw that the small Texan was coming in. Pausing only long enough to locate the center of the disturbance, he strolled over in the nonchalant fashion that often preceded a burst on his part into sudden action. For all his leisurely approach, his demeanor was that of one well used to dealing with a situation such as the one he found when he came to a halt at the gaming table where the gunplay had just taken place.

"Go fetch Doc Gottlinger from the Arizona State, please, Mr. Sinjun," Dusty ordered, after having glanced at each of the wounded men and turned his gaze to one of the occupants of the room he remembered by name. "Likely there's nobody *here* can 'tend to their needings."

"Sure, Cap'n Fog," the son of the town's butcher answered without hesitation. "I'll get him for you."

"I suppose you had a reason?" Dusty drawled, turning his attention to Eldridge when Garvin Sinjun had hurried away. "And you can put up that gun afore you start to tell it, mister."

"Depends what's called a reason around here," the pallid-faced Texan answered. As he was carrying out the order, he nodded toward the door. "Which I *allus* do what I'm told when there's good cause. Like now."

"Then tell it," Dusty commanded while everybody else looked over to where Rusty Willis had entered carrying a Greener ten-gauge shotgun at a position of readiness.

"Those two were playing together, and I'll bet it didn't just start after I sat in," Eldridge replied. He gave a nod toward Cutter, who was holding up the seven of diamonds retrieved from the floor where Glasser's chair had been. "Which I don't blame *you* for not spotting him, friend. They were mighty slick at it."

"Why didn't you say something?" the small Texan queried.

"I *did*," Eldridge answered. "Just as soon as I'd got something to show I wasn't a sore loser just spitting words to see how they flew."

"It was *them* as went for iron first, Sheriff," Cutter claimed. He was eager to show his gratitude for having been made to appear an innocent observer in the cheating. "Mr. Eldridge didn't have no other choice."

"And you took them both out, huh?" Dusty asked, apparently ignoring the houseman and directing the words at the other Texan. "You must be fast."

"I've never met nobody *faster*," Eldridge claimed.

There was an all-too-apparent note of challenge in the way the words were spoken. All the occupants of the barroom, Hatton in particular, waited to see whether it would be taken up by the blond Texan who was said to be the fastest gun in the West. Because of the amount of coverage gunfighting received, even in various articles and fictional stories appearing back east in periodicals such as the *Police Gazette,* there was a great interest in the results of gunfights and the kind of men whose names became prominent for engaging in them.

Not unexpectedly, therefore, everybody in the barroom shared Hatton's interest. Even those who did not know him personally or by mere acquaintance were aware of the reputation Dusty had acquired. While none could claim to have seen Eldridge before, they had witnessed the great speed with which he put down the two card cheats. No matter what the result, a confrontation between the pallid-faced Texan and the Rio Hondo gun wizard would be a sight to be remembered and boasted of ever after.

The crowd was to be disappointed.

"Cap'n Dusty!" Thorny Bush called, coming into the barroom in a hurry. "A feller's been found shot down by the livery barn!"

"I'll come," the small Texan replied, then turned his attention back to the man he was confronting. "Looks like you'd no choice but handle things the way you did, Mr. Eldridge. Only, I'd sooner you didn't make it a habit hereabouts."

"I only pull when I'm pulled on, Sheriff," the gambler replied. "How about the money on the table?"

"That's between you and the other gents in the game," Dusty answered, and turned to walk from the room with his deputies following him.

"Howdy, Mr. Eldridge," Hatton said, coming over as soon as the three Texans had left. "Me 'n' Steve Scott run the place. You did what needed doing, seeing as that pair were cheating. I reckon you and the rest of the players can share what they put into the game between you."

"That's the way I saw it," the Texan in gambler's clothes declared. "And I reckon these other gents agree."

165

"Come and take a drink with me," Hatton suggested after the division of the money had been carried out in accordance with the wishes of the players.

"Why, sure," Eldridge answered, and crossed to the bar with the New Englander. He would settle for a beer, he said, since he meant to play some more and never did that with hard liquor in him.

"I liked the way you handled things," Hatton asserted. "And there're some who'd reckon Dusty Fog didn't want no part of you, way he lit out of here."

"Neither of us wanted any truck with the other, fast as we both are," Eldridge corrected. "'Cause, should we go for our guns, the first out'll have lead headed his way afore his own can get there to stop it. Anyways, what've you got in mind besides buying me a drink?"

"In mind?"

"Hell, I know those two slippery-fingered bastards were working for the house. That's why I made it look like Cutter wasn't slick enough to catch them out."

"But—!" Hatton began, not knowing what to make of the Texan's words. He wished Scott were present to give guidance instead of taking pleasure with one of the saloon girls in the back room.

"From what I've seen around here," Eldridge stated, "you need somebody like me to run your gambling for you. I learned all I know from fellers like Last Card Johnny Bryan."

"I've heard of him," the New Englander

admitted. Scott had often spoken of the man as being an astute practitioner of crooked gambling.[1]

"He'd have laughed himself sick if he'd seen what I did while I was walking around your games," Eldridge drawled sardonically. " 'Cause those yahoos you've got handling wouldn't fool anybody who's even only half smart. Which, like I said, you need somebody as good as I am to show 'em the way afore you lose more of 'em the way you did just now."

15
THESE *ARE* MIGHTY FINE CIGARS

"We went 'round to where he's been staying, Dusty," Rusty Willis reported, coming into the sheriff's office after Thorny Bush and he had carried out a routine search of the boardinghouse where the victim was staying. "There wasn't anything in his room to say whether he'd been taken on by somebody here in town, and the lady who runs the place allowed he'd paid up for another week this morning."

En route with the deputies to the livery barn, Dusty Fog had learned that the victim had given his name as Jack Straw to Rusty and Bush when they met him, and to the owner of the boardinghouse where he was staying. He had been shot in the back by a heavy-caliber bullet about a hundred yards from the livery

---

1. How Last Card Johnny Bryan acquired his sobriquet is explained in Part One, "To Separate Innocence From Guilt," MORE J.T.'S LADIES.

barn, and if the position of his body was any guide, he was walking away from the gunman, not toward him. However, the small Texan had not discounted that the way the body was lying could have resulted from his having been spun around by the impact of the lead.

Rusty and Bush were given the task of searching the body with the aid of a lantern borrowed from the hostler on duty at the barn. Dusty questioned the hostler and the man who discovered the body. The latter said he had been on his way home from the Arizona State Saloon when he had heard the shot and had come to investigate. However, he had not seen anybody in the immediate vicinity, nor heard footsteps departing. The hostler said that, in addition to being somewhat hard of hearing, he was such a sound sleeper that he had not been disturbed by the shot; nor had he been awakened by a visitor to the barn. He also declared that he had never seen and did not even know if the dead man had a horse in the barn. The small Texan knew he did, but decided there was no point in trying to find out which animal it was.

When Dusty returned, the stocky Wedge hand reported that there was still over a hundred dollars on the body. They had agreed that this appeared to rule out robbery as the motive, unless the killer had taken flight on hearing the townsman approaching. The possibility of Straw having been gunned down as the result of an old enmity did not escape them. However, neither the victim nor anybody else had given any indication that this was the case.

Except for having sent Rusty and Bush to fetch the undertaker and arrange for the removal of the corpse, then go and examine the room at the boardinghouse where the victim was staying, Dusty had concluded that there had been nothing more to be done at the scene of the murder. There were several possible hiding places from which the shot could have been fired. However, even if the light given by the lantern had been sufficient for an examination of these to be made, the terrain underfoot was too hard to detect any tracks. The small Texan knew that Straw had not been on close terms with any of the other hired guns, because a watch had been kept by the deputies on all of them. He had only been seen in what appeared to be casual conversation with various of them, but he was never—to the deputies' knowledge—approached or openly contacted by anybody who lived in the town. Therefore, unless the search by the deputies brought something to light, nothing more could be done that night.

"We've fetched along everything he had in there," Rusty continued.

"You'll notice who had to do all the heavy toting?" Bush inquired, setting down the saddle he was carrying.

"That's what the youngest deputy is for," Dusty replied unsympathetically. "What do you make of his room, Rusty?"

"If he was figuring on lighting a shuck real sudden, there wasn't any sign of it," the stocky Wedge hand estimated. He directed a baleful glare at Bush as he went on, "I know he'd paid Mrs. Loften for another week, but that could

169

just've been a blind, 'fore some smart-alecky young sprout says so. Only, his spare duds were either in the wardrobe and or the drawers of the dressing table 'n' his washing 'n' shaving gear was laid out ready for morning on the washstand."

"Not a whole heap to show for a man's life, is there?" the youngster remarked somberly, looking at the garments and other items Rusty had carried.

"Not a whole heap," Dusty admitted.

"His clothes're better than most cowhands could afford, and that gun rig was built 'specially for him 'less I miss my guess," Rusty drawled. "He's likely never done him a day's hard work riding herd on cattle nor needed to live on cowhand's grub since he took on as a *pistolero,* and that wasn't yesterday. Top of which, he's sure got better smokings than I've ever managed to draw on, 'cepting maybe when Wedge paid off at the end of a drive."

"You're right," the small Texan said in a musing tone, as if speaking to himself, after he had opened one of the three tubes indicated by Rusty and examined its contents. Because two of his uncles, General Ole Devil Hardin and Judge Mannen Blaze, smoked such things, he was able to assess the quality of the thick brown cylinder of tobacco he was holding. "These *are* good cigars. Hold down the office, boys. I want to see a man."

After telling the two deputies to make a round of the town and look in on the Battling Belles Saloon to find out how seriously injured the two card cheats had been, Dusty took the cigar and its container with him as he left the jailhouse. Going to the Arizona State, he was pleased to see the man he wanted on the premises. Much to his satisfaction under the circumstances, somebody else he had asked to be there had arrived. However, he left going to see the latter party until he had dealt with the matter that had brought him to the barroom.

The small Texan had felt sure that the owner of Clitheroe's General Emporium was the most likely person in Child City to satisfy his curiosity. His establishment had been closed since sundown, but the man in question was taking advantage of the fact that his wife was attending some activity upon which the members of the Civic Betterment League were engaged with April Eardle. As the small Texan had anticipated, Amos Clitheroe was at the moment relaxing in the company of Counselor Edward Sutherland and the other prominent citizens who found themselves at liberty. On being asked by Angus McTavish whether he knew what the ladies were up to, he was able to state truthfully that he did not—despite his suspicions caused by the request Steffie Willis had made to the repentant losers on the morning after their fight.

After accepting a drink and briefly recounting the killing of Straw for the benefit of the attorney—the general consensus of opinion being that the death of a hired gun would be no great loss to the community—the small Texan made the request that had brought him to the barroom. He said he wanted the storekeeper to give an opinion on something, and as he had anticipated, was told this would be done without any questions asked. Going to a smaller table nearby—the rest of the prominent citizens struggling to affect an attitude of indifference—he showed Clitheroe what it was he wanted examined.

"You're right, Captain Fog," the store-keeper stated definitely after examining with the eye of a connoisseur the cigar and its tube. "This *is* very good. Cuban-rolled, and top-grade clear Havana leaf to boot."

"I sort of figured it wasn't from a barrel of long nine stogies rolled up quick and cheap in some Connecticut Valley," Dusty said with a grin that made him look younger than his years. He was referring to a variety of cigar that had for years been shipped to the West in large quantities despite its inferior quality. "Fact being, I'd reckon a man'd have to pay at least a quarter apiece for them."

"And the rest, which would be at least *double*." Clitheroe smiled, not fooled by the naive way the estimation of the price was made. "In fact—and I think this would be the answer to what you're figuring to ask next—they're so pricey I don't have any of them in the store. You'd have to go Prescott if you wanted anything this good, and I'd bet you won't find so many places that stock them on a regular basis even there."

"You couldn't say about when they were sold?"

"Not without examining the box they came from. Do you have it?"

"Nope," Dusty denied. "They were lying loose in a drawer at the place where the dead feller was staying."

"Then the best I can say is they've not been carried around for too long," the storekeeper estimated. "How long has he been around town?"

"Only a few days," the small Texan replied.

"Then I'd guess he'd come from Prescott," Clitheroe asserted confidently. "There's nowhere nearer he could have got them, and they haven't been bounced around in his thirty-year gatherings for as long as they've had to be if he'd got them anyplace else. Does that help you any?"

"I'm not for certain sure," the small Texan admitted, amused by the way in which the storekeeper had used the range term for a person's belongings. "Thanks for your help anyways, sir. I'm obliged for it."

"Think nothing of it," the storekeeper said cheerfully. "But, if you'd like to do me a favor in return, how about having one of your deputies sneak 'round and find out what our wives are up to?"

"Why, I'd be real pleased to oblige," Dusty claimed. "Only, I don't reckon it'd be the right 'n' proper thing for me to send them on anything that dangerous." Then he glanced to a group of soldiers occupying a table at the other side of the room and, although there was nothing to suggest a need for him to do so, he continued, "I reckon I'd best go warn Corporal Zmijewski to have his bunch hold down on the drinking and carousing, else they'll likely wind up learning how damned cold and drafty the jail is with the back wall still not mended."

"Howdy, Mr. Morris," Dusty Fog greeted as the door upon which he had knocked was opened. "I'm right pleased to have found you here. It saves me having to have you hunted up and taken from whatever you was doing."

"I have some paperwork I still have to catch up on despite having been at it ever since I closed the office," the agent for the Wells Fargo depot replied. He was in his shirt-sleeves and had removed both his collar and tie. Instead of allowing his visitor to enter the office building, he asked, "Why do you want to see me?"

"I've got to get a message sent to Prescott," the small Texan replied. He had decided against asking whether the man he had come to see had heard the shot that killed Jack Straw, since he considered this to be unlikely while the agent sat inside the sturdy walls of the company's main business building. "And it's out and away too important to be left until morning."

"But I've closed down the wire for the night, as there hasn't been anything to go out since sundown!" William Morris objected, his manner suggestive of annoyance over being interrupted in his work.

"Jim Hume allus told me that your telegraph offices are manned day and night," Dusty pointed out.

"They usually are," Morris admitted. "And this one would be, but the company hasn't been able to get anybody who can handle the telegraph key and is willing to come here, so there is only me to do it. Knowing this, the district supervisor told me when he sent me here that I need only send messages in an emergency after the main office has closed for the day."

"Well now, I reckon the message I have to have sent off right now counts as an emergency—or if it doesn't, I reckon it'll do for me until a real emergency drifts 'round," Dusty asserted, trying to look less intelligent than he was. "Seeing things from your point of view, I wouldn't want to have to pass word to your supervisor tomorrow that I couldn't have it sent tonight and the feller it's going to wouldn't be any too happy when he hears tell why it's been delayed getting to him."

"There won't be any need for that," Morris asserted without any noticeable enthusiasm as he moved aside to let the small Texan enter. He knew how James Hume always stressed the importance of cooperating in every way with the local peace officers, and he had decided he better avoid complaints for failing to do so. "Write out what you have to say and I'll send it."

"*Gracias*," the small Texan drawled. "I'm right obliged."

A short while later, Dusty leaned against the desk and watched while the agent read without apparent interest what was printed on one of the company's forms, even though it was addressed to the office of the United States marshal in Prescott and asked for most urgent inquiries to be made about where a certain brand of cigar could be obtained in the city and who had been recent purchasers. Asked if the subject

175

really was so important, the small Texan claimed with seeming veracity that a man's life could depend on the answer. Then, taking the form and a lamp, Morris went to the table beneath the window at the west side of the room and used the telegraph instrument positioned on it to dispatch the message. Regardless of his self-important demeanor, he handled the key and employed the Morse code used for transmitting the message with competence. When he was finished, there was a further clicking that he announced was the operator at the office in Prescott acknowledging receipt of the transmission.

"I'll have one of my deputies come down and wait for the reply," Dusty offered after paying for the service. "Knowing Matt as well as I do, it'll be taken straight to him and he'll get some of his boys on finding it out straightaway regardless of who gets woke up."

"It won't be necessary for you to take one of your men from his duties," Morris declared. He had a particular reason for not wishing to cause complaints from either James Hume or the U.S. marshal at this time, and had concluded that a display of willing assistance would not be amiss. "I've still got some work to do, and it will take me until the early hours in the morning to finish it. So if an answer comes before then, I'll fetch it to you. Do you want it brought to your office?"

"That'll do just dandy, 'n' it's real obliging of you," the small Texan affirmed. "There was a shooting fuss down to the Battling Belles earlier, and I want to have one of my deputies keep an eye on the tinhorn who did

176

it. The other's watching a bunch of bluebel-lies who've come in from Fort Mescalero to get rid of their pay as fast as they can drink it away. Thanks again, sir. I'm right sorry to've had to take you from your work, and I'll let you get back to it." Turning from the counter, he paused and looked over his shoulder. "Say, do you allus come to the door after dark without having a gun handy?"

"A *gun*? I've never used one in my life."

"It'd be useful to learn, 'case some owlhoot figures to rob you."

"He'd find poor pickings if he did," Morris claimed. "All the money and other valuables are put in the safe in my private office, and it has a time lock which can't be opened until nine o'clock in the morning. Do you think I should get a gun?"

"Not if you don't know how to use it real good," Dusty declared seriously. "A feller with a gun who doesn't know how to use it is more dangerous to hisself than anybody he fig-ures to use it on."

"I'll keep it in mind," the agent promised. He walked across the room to let the small Texan out, saying, "Good night, Sheriff. I'll fetch any message that arrives straight down to your office as soon as it comes in."

★ ★ ★

Returning to his private office after Dusty Fog had left the building and setting the lamp on the desk, William Morris drew open the drapes that had been closed when he left the office to answer the door. The he set about to give

177

the impression that he was engrossed in work on the papers in front of him. He continued in this fashion for almost an hour, then, after going to look out of the window, went into the main portion of the building. He opened the front door and stepped out, acting as if he was there for a breath of fresh air, and gazed about him. Then he set off along the front walk with steps suggesting he was stretching legs grown stiff from long hours at the desk. Turning the corner on the eastern side, he let out a low profanity as he saw a shape sprawled on the ground just below the nearer of the two windows. Going closer, he made the form out to be a soldier laying huddled and unmoving except for heavy breathing.

He delivered a less-than-gentle nudge in the ribs with his right Hersome gaiter boot, but failed to elicit the slightest response from the man at his feet. He bent closer and, when the smell of raw whiskey assailed his nostrils, he remembered what the small Texan had said about the party from Fort Mescalero drinking heavily at the Arizona State Saloon. Clearly this was one of them, and had decided, or been compelled, to take a walk in the hope of sobering up. From the way he continued to lie there, after having his shoulder shaken vigorously, there was not the slightest chance of this happening for some time. Giving a grunt of annoyance, Morris continued to walk around the building, scanning his surroundings carefully.

Back at his starting point, satisfied that there was only the drunken soldier in the vicinity, the agent entered the front door and locked it behind him. Going to the table by the east wall, he drew the drapes together before sitting down. Then he began to manipulate the key as swiftly and efficiently as he had previously. When he had got acknowledgment that the message had been received and understood at the office to which it had been dispatched, he gave a grunt of satisfaction. Coming to his feet and picking up the lamp, he went to his living quarters. Once inside, he changed into his night attire and, after dousing the light, got into bed.

16
HE'S *DUSTY FOG'S* COUSIN!

"He did what you said he might, Captain Fog," Corporal David Willets announced on entering the sheriff's office. Tall, slim, and good-looking, he had a voice like that of a man with a good education, and he was showing no sign of the intoxicated stupor that he had been simulating so competently outside the Wells Fargo depot about an hour earlier. Making a wry face, he sniffed distastefully at the borrowed uniform jacket that he had donned at the jailhouse prior to carrying out the assignment he was given at Fort Mescalero. "Whooee! If this is how you smell when you're drunk, I'm pleased that I'm a not a drinking man."

Even before the murder of Jack Straw, the small Texan had devised and made arrangements to put into effect a scheme whereby he hoped he would discover whether his theories regarding the complicity of William Morris were correct. The discoveries he had made about the cigars found among the hired gun's possessions had offered what he had considered to be a better reason for sending a telegraph message, which he hoped would provide the desired result. He had intended to put his plan into effect that night, and everything else was ready.

Taking advantage of a soldier who was riding dispatch to Fort Mescalero calling at the Arizona State Saloon for a beer, he had sent a message to the commanding officer requesting assistance. The quick compliance was helped by Colonel Claude de Tornay being a friend of long standing of Major Wilson Eardle. Earlier that afternoon, Corporals Willets and Antek Zmijewski had arrived in Child City with four enlisted men under the pretense of spending a pass. The former, one of the post's telegraph operators, soon satisfied Dusty that he could carry out the task required of him. After changing into the uniform of an enlisted man that was doused with cheap whiskey, Willets had gone to the Wells Fargo office while the small Texan was paying the visit and pretended to be in a drunken stupor when he was found by the agent. Then, having waited until the telegraph key was put to use, he had listened to the message with the aid of the base of a tumbler brought from the saloon and placed against the wall. When it was over, he had jotted down what was sent in the shorthand he had learned as an adjunct to his duties as a member of the Signal Corps. He waited until he was satisfied that the agent was asleep, then returned to the jailhouse to make his report.

"Here's what he sent," Willets said, opening the sheet of paper he carried in his hand. "It's addressed to the Titmus Land Development Trust at an address in Prescott and started "Urgent. Immediate Delivery." Then it says, 'Advise you end all negotiations with three companies soonest. Hiram Hickman.' Is that what you wanted to know?"

"You could say that," Dusty admitted. "My thanks, Corporal. I'll let Colonel de Tornay know in writing that you carried out the duty in a *most* satisfactory fashion."

★ ★ ★

"What's up?" James Knapp growled when William Morris signaled for him to come out of the livery barn at just after noon.

"We could be in bad trouble!" the Wells Fargo agent replied, putting down the locked carpetbag he was carrying. He had broken the rule of staying away during daylight hours from the man with whom he had been working for the so-called Titmus Land Development Trust. Their previous meetings had always taken place after dark when it was certain that nobody would see them together. He explained quickly about the message he had been compelled by Dusty Fog to dispatch the previous evening and the action he had taken as a result. "There was what I took to be a soldier sleeping off a drunk outside the office last night when I was sending to warn them. Only, when I saw him riding out with the others just now, he didn't show any signs of having been

181

drunk. What's more, he'd got on a corporal's jacket, not an enlisted man's and the facings of his uniform were buff, not yellow."

"So what?" the big, burly, unpleasant-looking owner of the barn growled, despite feeling worried over the way in which his normally unemotional senior co-conspirator was behaving.

"So that means he isn't Cavalry," Morris explained with the impatience he always showed when dealing with those low in the hierarchy of the so-called Titmus Land Development Trust who had been sent to coordinate matters in Spanish Grant County and remain ready for the takeover of the entire area. "Nor Infantry or Artillery either. In fact, I feel sure he's a telegraphist for the Signal Corps."

"So he's a tele—!" Knapp began, then realization struck home. "You mean the bastard could've heard and known what you sent to *them*?"

"Well, there couldn't be any other reason why he was there pretending to be in a drunken stupor, could there?" the agent pointed out sarcastically. "Damn it, I've always sensed Fog wasn't the country bumpkin that he pretended to be. He must have got onto me some way and fixed things up to find out if he was right or not."

"You mean he knows about you killing that hired gun those three bastards in Prescott sent to find out who was bringing in the others?" Knapp asked, looking worried.

"I don't think so," Morris answered, His ego did not permit him to admit that anybody— particularly a person whose manner of speech made appear him at best only slightly better than semi-illiterate and lacking his educational advantages—was intelligent enough to have outsmarted him. "He just used that as the reason for having me send a message he thought I'd feel needed to be passed on to *them* in Prescott. If it hadn't have been that, he'd have thought up something else to get the same effect."

"What're *you* figuring on doing?"

"Going to the Battling Belles."

"Now?" Knapp yelped, knowing that—like himself—the agent had only visited the saloon after dark, making certain not to be seen arriving. On the premises all negotiations had been carried out in the private office, with precautions taken to prevent anybody from entering or leaving.

"Now!" Morris affirmed, and opened his jacket to leave clear access to the butt of the Smith & Wesson Schofield Army Model of 1875 revolver which he had used to shoot Jack Straw in the back from hiding the previous evening.

"Why?" Knapp demanded, noticing the movement. He was aware that, although the agent might not have the speed of a Western *pistolero,* he was an excellent shot.

"Fog hasn't come near me yet, probably because he's waiting to hear from the U.S. marshal in Prescott," Morris replied after explaining the gist of the message he had sent to their superiors. "So I'm going to pull out before he does and I'm not going empty-handed or alone."

"I'll come with you," Knapp declared. "This whole deal's been falling apart at the

183

seams ever since that bitch of yours got caught robbing the bank."

"At least I made sure neither her husband or brother could tell Fog anything they knew," the agent pointed out, not troubling to try to refute the claim that he had had a clandestine relationship with Mrs. Harriet Harman that had led her to carry out the robbery earlier than was planned. "Jones said Harman kept hinting he knew something Fog would be interested in hearing, so his mouth had to be closed and the attempt at getting them both lynched fell through. Anyway, I think the time's come to get the hell away from here, as they will be doing in Prescott as soon as they've arranged to have those three bastards who loused up the deal with the ranches to be stopped talking *permanently* should arrests be made as a result of Fog's message, if I know *them*."

"I bet *that* was fixed up right after they got your warning," Knapp assessed, his always surly tone—which the man he was addressing had thought made him an unsuitable choice for an assistant when they first met—underlain with worry. "They're a cold-blooded bunch of bastards, that's for sure."

"That's why they're where they are and we're taking orders," Morris replied. "And you'd be better off staying here getting horses ready for us to get away on."

"Do you reckon so?" Knapp asked, his manner suspicious.

"I *do*," the agent stated, and put down the carpetbag. Without mentioning that it contained only some of his clothes, and that the money he had accrued from the embezzlement from the Cattlemen's Bank carried out by Mrs. Harman was in the wallet in his jacket's inside pocket, he went on, "Here, I'll leave this with you so you'll know I'll be back."

Walking away without giving Knapp time to reply, Morris went to the Battling Belles Saloon. However, his knock on the side door that gave access to the private office did not elicit any response, and he decided the urgency of the situation called for a relaxation of the usual precautions. He meant to leave town as soon as he had finished there, and he was only going in to ostensibly collect the cut of the business's profits their employers required from Derek Hatton and Steven Scott. With that in mind, he went around and through the batwing doors.

Upon entering, the agent glanced around and was pleased by what he saw. Because of the early hour, there were only employees and a few customers in the barroom, apart from the men he had come to call on. Among the customers were the six hired guns who had not moved on when hearing that the Ysabel Kid was riding the ranges where they should have been working to disrupt the roundup.

"Howdy, Mr. Morris," Hatton said. His manner less than cordial as he and Scott came across to greet Morris. They clearly considered him a less-than-welcome visitor. "What brings you here?"

"I've brought you a telegraph message from your suppliers in Prescott," Morris answered. "I think you'd better read it somewhere private and tell me if there's to be a reply."

"Hey, Der'," Scott remarked before he and his partner obeyed the order. "I hope Frenchie got paid for all the time she's been with him."

Following Scott's gaze, Morris saw a slender grizzled-brunette saloon girl come into the barroom accompanied by a tall and well-armed young Texan with fiery red hair. Then he realized the implications of Scott's words and concluded that the pair had started to run a sideline about which their employers were in ignorance. He concluded that he might be able to add to his traveling expenses by demanding a share of the proceeds. Before he could act on the thought, something happened that drove it from his mind.

"What's *he* doing here," demanded one of the hired guns, who the agent was unaware had not been present the day before when the man who called himself Charles Henry made his dramatic arrival.

"Who is he?" Scott called.

"His name's Red Blaze!" the hired gun answered, having stood up, his hand moving toward his holstered revolver. "He's Dusty Fog's cousin!"

Even as the declaration was being completed, the speaker brought his movements to a halt.

Although unable to recollect where their paths might have crossed, Charles Henry Blaze—the color of whose hair accounted for his sobriquet—guessed what was coming. Gently shoving away Fifi le Planchet, his hands turned outward to bring the long-barreled Cavalry Model Peacemakers from leather, preventing the hired gun's attempted draw. His other weapon swung in a menacing arc, ready to counter trouble from elsewhere in the room. But he failed to see the gun being brought from the waistband of one of the bouncers.

"Leave it there!" demanded a voice with a Texas drawl before the second attempt against the redhead could be completed.

The gambler who had introduced himself as Marvin Eldridge was watching from where he stood at a nearby chuck-a-luck table, idly turning the "birdcage" device in which the game's three dice were rolled. As he gave the order, his right hand made another sight-defying motion that brought the ivory-butted Civilian Model Peacemaker out, ready for use.

"*Gracias,* Doc!" Red Blaze thanked without bothering to find out the reason for the order. "Let's everybody stay good and still!"

"I couldn't've put it better, Red," the pallid-faced Texan commented. "Do you reckon we could have outstayed our welcome a mite?"

"That I do, good buddy, that I do," the cousin of Dusty Fog confirmed. "Which being, we'd best be saying, 'Bye now, you-all' to these good folks and light a shuck for friendly places."

"Can I come with you?" Fifi inquired, not caring for the coldly hostile way in which Hatton and Scott were glowering at her.

"Why, surely so," Red answered. "How could I refuse a lovely lady like you after the night we've spent together?"

The telegraph message sent to Maisie Randal in Backsight, with the instruction to try elsewhere and not at any of the local ranches, the apparent mistakes in the way it was addressed, and the use of the names "Charles Henry" and "Marvin Eldridge" had told the pair what Dusty wanted them to do. Given permission to carry out the assignment by his wife, the former Sue Ortega, Red and his companion—who was using his given name and had the necessary skill and knowledge of cheating methods for various games of chance, and was exceptionally fast with a gun—came to Child City ready to play their part. Meeting with the small Texan where they would not be observed, they had learned what April Eardle had arranged. It was decided that Red would be the one to make contact with Fifi to find out if she could tell them anything of use.

A gurgle of amusement had come from the grizzled-brunette when she heard the reason for her being allowed to accompany the two Texans. After they had left the saloon the previous afternoon, she had escorted "Charlie Henry" on a stroll around the shopping area of town. Her instincts could not resist the temptation to point out a hat in the window given over to feminine attire at Clitheroe's General Emporium and say—in a tone that reached the ears of a couple of "good" women close by—that she would surely like to have one that fancy. Mainly to bolster the reasons given for their departure from the saloon should anybody be following them, Red had taken her inside and purchased it. To further help pass the time, they had taken baths in the facilities provided for members of their respective sexes in the Summers Hotel. Red had taken the opportunity to get a shave and have his travel-stained clothes made more presentable.

At the boardinghouse where she and the other female employees of the Battling Belles Saloon were accommodated, they had availed themselves of the owner's offer of a small cabin to the rear of the house. The cabin afforded them greater privacy than would the room she shared with Doxie Rimmer.

What happened next had been a complete surprise to Fifi. When she hinted that he might as well have his money's worth, "Charlie" replied that he was a happily married man and, with a broad grin, said he was sure his good lady, Sue, would not take kindly to him doing as was suggested. The grizzled-brunette had admitted, while they were preparing to go for a late breakfast in the dining room of the Summers Hotel that morning, that she never thought she would receive payment for spending the early part of a night playing cribbage with a man, then have him sleep on the floor instead of with her in bed.

"Hellfire!" exclaimed the hired gun who had talked with Scott about "Marvin Eldridge" the day before. The Texans had backed out of the barroom, following Fifi through the batwing doors that she held open for them. "*Now* I know who he is!"

"Who?" the Illinoisian asked, the words having been directed his way.

"The way that coat was stitched back should've told me," the man answered. "Only, he's never been a gambler afore."

"Who is he, damn it!" Hatton snarled.

"They call him Doc Leroy," the hired gun answered. "And he used to ride for Stone Hart's Wedge, then with Ole Devil Hardin's floating outfit."

"Hey, boss!" the bouncer who had been prevented from drawing his gun yelled, having crossed to a window. "They've met up with Dusty Fog and his deputies outside. Going by the scatters the deputies are toting, they've come loaded for bear."

"All right, Mr. Morris!" shouted a voice most of the room's occupants recognized as that of the Rio Hondo gun wizard. "Come on out with your hands held high."

"Why not try to *make* us?" the agent shouted back. "We're all in it together, and you want *them* as well as me!"

"You *bastard*—!" Hatton snarled, then gulped as he looked into the barrel of the heavy-caliber Smith & Wesson that was being pointed at him.

"Shut your mouth and do as I do!" Morris commanded. Striding across the room, he caught Doxie Rimmer by the arm, placed the muzzle of his weapon against her head, and snarled, "Stand still, the rest of you bitches. Get one of them each, all of you." When the order was obeyed, he yelled, "Fog, we've all got a gun apiece on the women. Leave your gunbelts and the shotguns on the street and then move right away from them. Do it *fast.* I'll count to ten, and if you've not done it, I'll blow her brains out for starters. Then the rest will go one at a time until you move."

17
COME ON, WEDGE!

"All right," Dusty Fog said, starting to remove his gunbelt. He had no doubt that the threat would be carried out and, as he knew was true of his companions in front of the Battling Belles saloon, he did not wish the death of any of the saloon girls on his conscience. "Do like he says!"

Watching from the window, a firm grip on Doxie Rimmer's arm with his left hand and the muzzle of his Smith & Wesson revolver touching her temple, William Morris felt a surge of elation as he watched the Texans do as he had told them. He had gambled successfully on their Southern upbringing preventing them from endangering the lives of women, even saloon workers. Satisfied that he had achieved his purpose, he glanced around. Steven Scott was holding and covering Winnie Ashwell, and at other points in the barroom, four of the hired guns were in possession of the remaining saloon girls. The local loafers were sitting rigid on their chairs, clearly wishing they were anywhere except there. Waiting until the now-disarmed Texans were too far along the street for any who may have been carrying a concealable weapon to pose a threat, he changed his hold on the little blonde so his left arm was across her throat and he would be partially hidden behind her buxom body.

"All right," the Wells Fargo agent barked. "Let's get going. They won't dare do anything as long as we've got these bitches for shields, so we'll get our horses and head out as fast as we can ride."

"Let me go empty the box!" Scott suggested, thinking of the money held in the safe in the private office.

"You go ahead," Morris answered. "But I'm doing what I said straightaway. Who's coming with me?"

Even the hired guns who did not have a human shield assented, so Scott reluctantly decided he would accompany them. However, as they began to follow the man they now accepted as their leader, Derek Hatton did not move forward. Instead, he turned and made his way stealthily toward the door of the private office. He was aware that the safe could be opened only by using two keys, one of which was always in his possession, the other held by his partner. However, unbeknownst to Scott, Hatton had had a duplicate made of Scott's key and would be able to gain access to the money held in the safe. With the money in his possession, he intended to compel Counselor Nigel Jones to hide him until he could make good his escape. He felt that an offer of a share of the loot would convince Jones to comply.

"Go and get their guns!" Morris ordered as he and the other men forced their hostages ahead of them onto the street.

Eager to obtain the superlative gunbelts left behind by the Texans, the two unprotected hired guns moved ahead of the others to do as commanded. They could see that Dusty Fog and the others were well away, although Fifi le Planchet had for some reason halted by the end of the saloon and was looking at them in a distinctly hostile fashion. Before they could decide why she was behaving in such a manner, instead of having gone to safety, they were supplied with the answer.

"You lousy *bastard*!" the slender grizzled-brunette screeched in a furious voice, starting to run forward.

"Come on, Wedge!" a baritone voice with a Texas drawl thundered from an alley across the street as Fifi was speaking.

Guessing a showdown might erupt as a result of his activities the previous night, particularly since he had had Corporal David Willets be seen by Morris with instructions to ensure that the part of the drunken soldier become known—which had not proved necessary due to the agent's keen powers of observation—the small Texan had known he would need more than the assistance offered by his deputies, Red Blaze, and Doc Leroy to deal with it, competent as all had proved themselves to be. He had had no wish to put at risk the lives of the local businessmen, most of whom were married. Instead, he had secured the services of Wendel Debutson to fetch supporters with no marital ties. Sensing the possibility that a story of such magnitude might bring him to the attention of a major newspaper, perhaps even outside Arizona, he had willingly ridden to the roundup bunch ground.

On hearing the news, Jimmy Conlin, speaking in his capacity as straw boss, had said he felt the entire Wedge crew had the right to answer the summons from Dusty. That had included even the men on guard duty at the ranch house, who could be replaced by members from the other spreads. Hard riding had brought the reinforcements to town in the early hours of the morning, and they had taken up their positions before the arrival of the three temporary lawmen.

Seeing Mark burst into view with a Cavalry Model Peacemaker in each hand, other armed Texans making their appearances from other points, Doxie proved she was not the featherheaded little blonde she gave the impression of being. Grabbing the arm across her throat, she raised it until she could sink her teeth into the hand. Then, she gave a surging twist of her buxom body, which obtained her liberty. Showing a very good grasp of the situation, she threw herself to alight facedown on the street. The revolver crashed close behind her, but the bullet did not come anywhere near.

The remainder of the saloon girls were equally successful in avoiding the fate with which they were threatened. Wrenching away from Scott, who was too surprised to do anything about stopping her, Winnie drove a knee into his groin as hard as she could manage, then followed Doxie's example and got out of the way of the gunfire she knew was coming. Nor—possibly because they were aware of what their fate would be if taken alive after having killed a woman in such circumstances—did any of three hired guns who had acquired hostages fare any better. The women Morris and the

Illinoisian were holding simply jerked free, then dropped to the surface of the street.

With their human protective shields gone, Morris and the men with him were faced by a situation they had not envisaged.

Letting out a snarl of fury as he realized that his hope of making good an escape would be increased once he was able to contact the men who had employed him, the agent started to swing around his Smith & Wesson. Alongside Mark was the Ysabel Kid, clad all in black as usual but with none of the babyish innocence his Indian-dark handsome face showed in repose—rather, looking as dangerous and totally ruthless as the Pehane Comanche warrior he had been trained in childhood to be. The Ysabel Kid began to shoot with the magnificent Winchester "One of a Thousand" Model of 1873 rifle he had won at the first Cochise County Fair, showing the speed and accuracy for which he was famous.[1] Caught in the flying spread of bullets, Morris was thrown from his feet and landed dead before he had been able to operate the double-action mechanism of his revolver.

Holding his groin with his left hand while mumbling profanities, Scott tried to avenge himself. Even as the barrel of his Merwin & Hulbert Army Pocket revolver was slanting down at Winnie, Mark cut loose with his Colts to put three bullets—any of which would have proved fatal—into him to bring his actions to a halt.

Watching the approaching Texans and real-

1. Told in GUN WIZARD.

izing their deep sense of purpose, five of the hired guns knew there was not a hope of fighting them off. Doubting whether their connection with any of the illegal activities upon which they had engaged could be proved, the quintet discarded their weapons and yelled their surrender. However, the sixth man, knowing he was on a wanted poster for a killing carried out at Tucson, had no desire to be taken into custody. He sent a shot that dropped Silent Churchman with a bad graze across the thigh. Instantly, Peaceful Gunn and Dude opened fire in return. The hired gun was dead before he measured his length on the hard-packed dirt surface of the street.

"Go take a look inside, Mark," Dusty ordered, returning with the rest of the disarmed party to collect their weapons. "There's another of the big chiefs in there and I want him—alive to do some talking—if he wants it that way."

"Yo!" the blond giant assented as the pallid-faced Texan went to where the wounded Silent Churchman lay on the ground with the intention of attending to the wound with the medical skill that had produced his sobriquet, although he had not yet qualified as a medical practitioner. "Coming, Lon?"[2]

"I might as well," the black-clad Texan answered. "I for sure don't want to have to listen to Doc bellyaching 'bout how he allus winds up 'tending to somebody's hurts every time he gets into a gunfight like he allus does."

2. How Marvin Eldridge Leroy became a qualified doctor is told in DOC LEROY, M.D.

Going into the saloon with weapons drawn, Mark and the Kid found there was no need to defend themselves. Neither the employees nor the local loafers offered any resistance. Cutter pointed to the door of the private office and said they would find the man they were looking for inside. They went over, and a kick from the blond giant's right foot sprung the lock and allowed them to gain admittance. Crouching before the safe, Hatton twisted around and reached for the Colt Peacemaker that he had placed on the roof of the safe. However, confronted by the two Colts and the Winchester that were immediately lined his way, he raised his hands and surrendered.

"It wouldn't done you not a li'l bit of good had you sneaked out with all the money like you was planning," the Kid informed the New Englander cheerfully. "There's good ole Counselor Sutherland, Angus McTavish, and some more gents who wouldn't be left out of things, waiting with ten-gauges all loaded up with buckshot to stop anybody who tried to do just that."

★   ★   ★

The death of William Morris brought an end to the troubles that had plagued Spanish Grant County since the arrival at their new home of the Wedge's owner, wife, and crew. Questioned by Dusty Fog, Derek Hatton and James Knapp—the latter arrested by Rusty Willis and Thorny Bush as he was preparing to leave the livery barn on the best of its horses—could do more than fill in a few details of the various incidents that had taken place.

The owner of the livery barn claimed that the attempt to abduct Margaret Hart, which was thwarted by herself and Dusty, was made without the knowledge of either Morris or himself. However, Knapp declared that his superior had conspired with Harriet Harman to embezzle money from the Cattlemen's Bank and use the robbery that was attempted to cover up their crime. From what he learned, the small Texan realized that there had been two factions striving for the same goal without more than a nominal cooperation, despite both being in the employ of somebody with whom only the Wells Fargo agent in Child City had ever been in personal contact. Hatton explained how Morris had planned for the mob to be induced to carry out the lynching of Robin C. Harman and Cuthbert Castle in a way that would also remove Dusty, whose abilities as a lawman had caused too many schemes to go wrong and threatened to continue to do so. It was hoped that having Fay kill him would cause the men in the crowd to attack the jailhouse, believing that they had been fired upon, and hang the prisoners.

Acting upon the message sent by the small Texan, the United States marshal in Prescott had discovered to whom some of the expensive cigars had been sold. However, Anthony Blair, Willis Norman, and Graeme Steel were found murdered by the local law-enforcement officers; it appeared that a robbery at the house where they were hiding was their undoing. A visit by the U.S. marshal to the address given by Morris for the Titmus Land Development Trust found the office empty, and nobody could say where the occupants had gone. Nor was anybody connected to it traced. The documents purporting to establish that the two ranches had been left by Edgar Eustace Eisteddfod and Patrick Hayes to kinsmen were forgeries, and, wishing to avoid further problems, the governor ordered that they be sold to Stone Hart and Major Wilson Eardle.

There were positive developments at Child City in the aftermath of the failed plot. Wishing to save Spanish Grant County from the expense incurred by trials—in which establishing the guilt of Hatton or Knapp for any of the crimes would prove impossible—Counselor Sutherland acting in his capacity as justice of the peace for the area, had given both men an opportunity to leave Child City, which they were only too pleased to accept. Having what would pass as legal proof that he was part owner of the Battling Belles Saloon, the New Englander sold it to McTavish—who ran it in behalf of the church and school after Doc Leroy removed the cheating devices from its gambling games and the employees were given the choice of behaving honestly or quitting and going—for a nominal sum. The New Englander was allowed to leave town.

The money from the safe was added to that retrieved from Morris's body and the result of a similar deal involving Knapp to help bring the Cattlemen's Bank back to solvency. While the arrangement might not have been in strict accordance with the law, when hearing of it in confidence, the governor had stated that such a thing must never happen again, then elevated the attorney to the status of Judge as an indication of his unofficial approval. By order of the Territorial Legislature, the bank was put in trustworthy hands and was reopened.

Things were soon back to normal through the county.

Although it took longer than intended—there being much rebranding of Vertical Triple E and Arrow P cattle to the marks of their new ownership—the roundup proved a great success. Its conclusion was celebrated by the production of the show put on by the ladies of the Civic Betterment of Child City League under the guidance of April Eardle. It was quite a surprise for the audience. In addition to the blonde's songs from her career before she was "saved from a life of sin," she had some of the town's most eminent "good" women, clad in borrowed saloon girl attire, perform a high-kick dance declared to be the height of the evening's entertainment. The affair proved such a success that it became an annual event and attained great fame that everybody who considered themselves anybody, including successive governors and their wives, insisted upon attending.

One person expressed misgivings over a certain aspect of the way the men concerned were brought to justice. The injury sustained by Silent subsequently proved to be a further source of annoyance for Rosita Martinez. It was decided that the need for guards was no longer necessary, and the rest of the guards were able to join the roundup crew. However,

Silent was unable to do so because of the stitches with which the wound was secured. This meant he was able to keep a careful eye on the calf that he had saved from a black bear sow—the number and variety of dangerous would-be assailants growing every time he told the story—while on the trail drive to the ranch. Regardless of his frequent protestations that he hated "cows" of every description, he insisted she be treated as a special charge in her capacity of custodian of such young creatures as had been abandoned by their mothers.[3] He was, Rosita had often complained, far worse than any proud father with whom she had been acquainted.

With their part in the cleaning up of Child City completed, Red Blaze and Doc Leroy returned to Backsight. The former told his wife of the way he had spent the night with Fifi le Planchet, and she laughingly stated that she did not mind, since she trusted him and knew he was too danged scared of what she would have done if he had misbehaved.

Doc Leroy had been the source of some mock hostile comments from the youngest member of Ole Devil Hardin's floating outfit. Waco had sustained a serious wound at the conclusion of some trouble in the town and, having been kept alive by the prompt attention he received from Doc, was still not fully recovered.[4] Therefore, much to his loudly expressed disgust, he had been refused permission to accompany his two *amigos* in response to the

3. Told in WEDGE GOES TO ARIZONA.
4. Told in RETURN TO BACKSIGHT.

message sent by Dusty. His objections had been stifled by Sue Blaze and her equally determined sister-in-law, Louise Ortega, who had hidden all his outdoor clothes and threatened to sit on his chest if he tried to leave his bed.

With Sheriff Amon Reeves sufficiently recovered from his injury to return to at least supervisory duty, Dusty had been able to resume his duties as roundup captain—a change the cowhands had jokingly asserted was like finding the grippe one thought one was suffering from was really a more malignant disease—and held this post until the gathering of the stock was finished. At the request of the men, who claimed their profane vocabulary was being vastly curtailed, April had kept the tally book as often as her duties as manager for the ladies' show in Child City permitted.

Knowing Margaret was now sufficiently used to the ranch house and its surroundings not to require her assistance any longer, Steffie Willis had given consideration to accepting an offer from Doctor Klaus Gottlinger—claiming it was a task he had always hated—to become his midwife and attendant for female patients. Her decision to do so was made possible by Rusty and Bush having been asked by Reeves to remain as permanent deputy sheriffs. They had agreed after they had discussed the matter with Stone Hart on his return from Prescott. Hart had replaced them as full-time members of the Wedge ranch's crew by persuading Dude and a Welsh cowhand who had impressed him as a hard and competent worker on the trail drive from Texas to stay on.

Peace had been brought to Spanish Grant County and the roundup was over. Although Red and Doc had to return to Backsight, Dusty, Mark, and the Kid set off on their return to the OD Connected ranch, where they expected there would be some other kind of work awaiting their attention. They left secure in the knowledge that Stone Hart and his loyal Wedge crew had at last attained a home.

Appendix One

Following his enrollment in the Army of the Confederate States,[1] by the time he reached the age of seventeen, Dustine Edward Marsden "Dusty" Fog had won promotion in the field to the rank of captain and was put in command of Company "C," Texas Light Cavalry.[2] At the head of them throughout the campaign in Arkansas he had earned the reputation for being an exceptional military raider and worthy contemporary of Turner Ashby and John Singleton "the Gray Ghost" Mosby, the South's other leading exponents of what would later become known as "commando" raids.[3] In addition to averting a scheme by a Union general to employ a virulent version of what was to be given the name "mustard gas" following its use by Germans in World War I[4] and preventing a pair of pro-Northern fanatics from starting an Indian uprising that would have decimated much of Texas,[5] he had supported Belle "the Rebel Spy" Boyd on two of her most dangerous assignments.[6]

At the conclusion of the War Between the States, Dusty became the *segundo* of the great OD Connected ranch its brand being a letter *O* to which was attached a *D* in Rio Hondo County, Texas. Its owner and his maternal uncle, General Jackson Baines "Ole Devil" Hardin, CSA, had been crippled in a riding accident and was confined to a wheelchair.[7] This placed much responsibility, including the need to handle an important mission with the future relationship between the United States and Mexico at stake upon his young shoulders.[8] While carrying out the assignment, he met Mark Counter and the Ysabel Kid, *q.v.* Not only did they do much to bring it to successful conclusion, they became his closest friends and leading lights of the ranch's floating outfit.[9] After helping to gather horses to replenish the ranch's depleted *remuda*,[10] he was sent to assist Colonel Charles Goodnight[11] on the trail drive to Fort Sumner, New Mexico, which did much to help Texas recover from the impoverished conditions left by the War.[12] With that achieved, he had been equally successful in helping Goodnight convince other ranchers that it would be possible to drive large herds of longhorn cattle to the railroad in Kansas.[13]

Having proved himself to be a first-class cowhand, Dusty went on to become acknowledged as a very competent trail boss,[14] roundup captain,[15] and town-taming lawman.[16] Competing in the first Cochise County Fair in Arizona, against a number of well-known exponents of very rapid drawing and accurate shooting with revolvers, he won the title "The Fastest Gun in the West."[17] In later years, following his marriage to Lady Winifred Amelia "Freddie Woods" Besgrove-Woodstole,[18] he became a noted diplomat.

Dusty never found his lack of stature an impediment to achievement. In fact, he occasionally found that it helped him to achieve a purpose.[19] To supplement his natural strength,[20] also perhaps with a desire to distract attention from his small size, he had taught himself to be completely ambidextrous.[21] Possessing perfectly attuned reflexes, he could draw either, or both, his Colts whether the 1860 Army Model[22] or their improved "descendant," the fabled 1873 Model "Peacemaker"[23] with lightning speed and shoot most accurately. Furthermore, Ole Devil Hardin's "valet," Tommy Okasi, was Japanese and a trained *samurai* warrior.[24] From him, as was the case with the General's "granddaughter," Elizabeth "Betty" Hardin,[25] Dusty learned jujitsu and karate. Neither form of unarmed combat had received the publicity they would be given in later years and were little known in the Western Hemisphere at that time. Therefore. Dusty found the knowledge useful when he had to fight with bare hands against larger, heavier, stronger men.

1. *Details of some of Dustine Edward Marsden "Dusty" Fog's activities prior to his enrollment are given in Part Five, "A Time for Improvisation, Mr. Blaze,"* J.T.'S HUNDREDTH.

2. *Told in* YOU'RE IN COMMAND NOW, MR. FOG.

3. *Told in* THE BIG GUN, UNDER THE STARS AND BARS, *Part One, "The Futility of War,"* THE FASTEST GUN IN TEXAS, *and* KILL DUSTY FOG!

4. *Told in* A MATTER OF HONOUR.

5. *Told in* THE DEVIL GUN.

6. *Told in* THE COLT AND THE SABRE *and* THE REBEL SPY.

6a. *More details of the career of Belle "the Rebel Spy" Boyd can be found in* MISSISSIPPI RAIDER; BLOODY BORDER; RENEGADE THE HOODED RIDERS; THE BAD BUNCH; SET A-FOOT; TO ARMS! TO ARMS! IN DIXIE!;

THE SOUTH WILL RISE AGAIN; THE QUEST FOR BOWIE'S BLADE; Part Eight, "Affair Of Honour," J.T.'S HUNDREDTH, *and* Part Five, "The Butcher's Fiery End," J.T.'S LADIES.

7.   *Told in Part Three, "The Paint,"* THE FASTEST GUN IN TEXAS.

7a.   *Further information about the General's earlier career is given in the Ole Devil Hardin and Civil War series. His death is recorded in* DOC LEROY, M.D.

8.   *Told in* THE YSABEL KID.

9.   *"Floating outfit": a group of four to six cowhands employed by a large ranch to work the more distant sections of the property. Taking food in a chuck wagon, or "greasy sack" on the back of a mule, they would be away from the ranch house for long periods and so were selected for their honesty, loyalty, reliability, and capability in all aspects of their work. Because of General Hardin's prominence in the affairs of Texas, the OD Connected's floating outfit were frequently sent to assist such of his friends who found themselves in difficulties or endangered.*

10.   *Told in* .44 CALIBRE MAN *and* A HORSE CALLED MOGOLLON.

11.   *Rancher and master cattleman Charles Goodnight never served in the Army. The rank was honorary and granted by his fellow Texans out of respect for his abilities as a fighting man and leader.*

11a. *In addition to playing an active part in the events recorded in the books referred to in Footnotes 13 and 14, Colonel Goodnight makes "guest" appearances in Part One, "The Half Breed,"* THE HALF BREED, *its "expansion,"* WHITE INDIANS, *and* IS-A-MAN.

11b. *Although Dusty Fog never received higher official rank than Captain, in the later years of his life he,*

208

too, was given the honorific "Colonel" for possessing the same qualities.

12. *Told in* GOODNIGHT'S DREAM *Bantam Books, USA, July 1974 edition retitled* THE FLOATING OUTFIT, *despite our already having had a volume of that name published by Corgi Books, UK, see Footnote 9 and* FROM HIDE AND HORN.

13. *Told in* SET TEXAS BACK ON HER FEET *although Berkley Books, New York, retitled it for their October 1978 edition* VIRIDIAN'S TRAIL, *they reverted to the original title when reissuing the book in July 1980 and* THE HIDE AND TALLOW MEN.

14. *Told in* TRAIL BOSS.

15. *Told in* THE MAN FROM TEXAS.

16. *Told in* QUIET TOWN; THE MAKING OF A LAWMAN, THE TROUBLE BUSTERS, DECISION FOR DUSTY FOG, CARDS AND COLTS, THE CODE OF DUSTY FOG, THE GENTLE GIANT, THE SMALL TEXAN, *and* THE TOWN TAMERS.

17. *Told in* GUN WIZARD.

18. *Lady Winifred Besgrove-Woodstole appears as "Freddie Woods" in* THE TROUBLE BUSTERS; THE MAKING OF A LAWMAN; THE GENTLE GIANT; BUFFALO ARE COMING!; THE FORTUNE HUNTERS; WHITE STALLION, RED MARE; THE WHIP AND THE WAR LANCE; *and Part Five, "The Butcher's Fiery End,"* J.T.'S LADIES. *She also "guest stars" under her married name, Mrs. Freddie Fog, in* NO FINGER ON THE TRIGGER *and* CURE THE TEXAS FEVER.

19. *Three occasions when Dusty Fog utilized his small size to his advantage are described in* KILL

209

DUSTY FOG!; *Part One, "Dusty Fog and the Schoolteacher,"* THE HARD RIDERS; *its "expansion,"* TRIGGER MASTER; *and Part One, "The Phantom of Gallup Creek,"* THE FLOATING OUTFIT.

20.   *Two examples of how Dusty Fog exploited his exceptional physical strength are given in* TRIGGER MASTER *and* THE PEACEMAKERS.

21.   *The ambidextrous prowess was in part hereditary. It was possessed and exploited with equal success by Freddie and Dusty's grandson, Alvin Dustine "Cap" Fog, who also inherited his grandfather's Hercules-in-miniature physique. Alvin utilized these traits to help him become acknowledged as one of the finest combat pistol shots in the United States during the Prohibition era and to earn his nickname becoming the youngest man ever to hold rank of Captain in the Texas Rangers. See the Alvin Dustine "Cap" Fog series for further details of his career.*

22.   *Although the military sometimes claimed derisively that it was easier to kill a sailor than a soldier, the weight factor of the respective weapons had caused the United States Navy to adopt a .36-caliber revolver, while the Army employed the larger .44. The reason was that the weapon would be carried on a seaman's belt and not handguns having been originally and primarily developed for use by cavalry on the person or saddle of a man who would be doing most of his traveling and fighting from the back of a horse. Therefore, the .44 became known as the "Army" calibre, and the .36, the "Navy."*

23.   *Details about the Colt Model of 1873, more commonly known as the "Peacemaker," can be found in those volumes following* THE PEACEMAKERS *on our list of titles in chronological sequence for the Floating Outfit Series.*

24.   "Tommy Okasi" is an Americanized corruption of the name given by the man in question, who had left Japan for reasons that the Hardin, Fog, and Blaze families refuse to divulge even at this late date, when he was rescued from a derelict vessel in the China Sea by a ship under the command of General Hardin's father.

25.   The same members of the Hardin, Fog, and Blaze families cannot or will not make any statement on the exact relationship between Elizabeth "Betty" and her "grandfather," General Hardin.

25a.   Betty Hardin appears in Part Five, "A Time for Improvisation, Mr. Blaze," J.T.'S LADIES; KILL DUSTY FOG!; THE BAD BUNCH; McGRAW'S INHERITANCE; TRIGGER MASTER; Part Two, "The Quartet," THE HALF BREED; its "expansion," TEXAS KIDNAPPERS; THE RIO HONDO WAR, and GUN-SMOKE THUNDER.

Appendix Two

With his exceptional good looks and magnificent physical development,[1] Mark Counter presented the kind of appearance many people expected of a man with the reputation gained by his *amigo*, Captain Dustine Edward Marsden "Dusty" Fog. It was a fact of which they took advantage when the need arose.[2] On one occasion, it was also the cause of the blond giant being subjected to a murder attempt, although the Rio Hondo gun wizard was the intended victim.[3]

While serving as a lieutenant under the command of General Bushrod Sheldon in the

War Between the States, Mark's merits as an efficient and courageous officer had been over-shadowed by his unconventional taste in uniforms. Always something of a dandy, coming from a wealthy family had allowed him to indulge in his whims. Despite considerable opposition and disapproval from hide-bound senior officers, his adoption of a "skirtless" tunic in particular had come to be much copied by the other rich young bloods of the Confederate States Army.[4] Similarly in later years, having received an independent income through the will of a maiden aunt, his taste in attire had dictated what the well-dressed cowhand from Texas would wear to be in fashion.

When peace had come between the North and the South, Mark had accompanied Sheldon to fight for Emperor Maximilian in Mexico. There he had met Dusty Fog and the Ysabel Kid. On returning with them to Texas, he had received an offer to join the floating outfit of the OD Connected ranch. Knowing that his two older brothers could help his father, Big Ranse, to run the family's R Over C ranch in the Big Ben country and considering life would be more enjoyable and exciting in the company of his two *amigos* he accepted.

An expert cowhand, Mark had become known as Dusty's right bower. He had also gained acclaim by virtue of his enormous strength. Among other feats, it was told how he used a treetrunk in the style of a Scottish caber to dislodge outlaws from a cabin in which they had forted up,[5] and broke the neck of a Texas longhorn steer with his bare hands. He had acquired further fame for his ability at barehanded roughhouse brawling. However, due to spending so much time in the company of the Rio Hondo gun wizard, his full potential as a gunfighter received little attention. Nevertheless, men who were competent to judge such matters stated that he was second only to the small Texan when it came to drawing fast and shooting accurately with a brace of long-barreled Colt revolvers.

Many women found Mark irresistible, including Martha "Calamity Jane" Canary.[6] However, in his younger days, only one the lady outlaw Belle Starr held his heart.[7] It was not until several years after her death that he courted and married Dawn Sutherland, whom he had first met on the trail drive taken by Colonel Charles Goodnight to Fort Sumner, New Mexico.[8] The discovery of oil on their ranch brought an added wealth to them, and this commodity now produces the major part of the income of the present members of the family.[9]

Recent biographical details we have received from the current head of the family, Andrew Mark "Big Andy" Counter, establish that Mark was descended on his mother's side from Sir Reginald Front de Boeuf, notorious as the lord of Torquilstone Castle in medieval England[10] and lived up to the family motto, "Cave Adsum."[11] However, the blond giant had not inherited the very unsavory character and behavior of his ancestor, although a maternal aunt and her son, Jessica and Trudeau Front de Boeuf, behaved in a way that suggested they had done so.[12]

1.   *Two of Mark Counter's grandsons, Andrew Mark "Big Andy" Counter and Ranse Smith, inherited his good looks and exceptional physique, as did two great-grandsons, Deputy Sheriff Bradford "Brad" Counter and James Allenvale "Bunduki" Gunn. Unfortunately, while willing to supply information about other members of his family, past and present, "Big Andy" has so far declined to allow publication of any of his own adventures.*

1a.   *Some details of Ranse Smith's career as a peace officer during the Prohibition era are recorded in* THE JUSTICE OF COMPANY "Z," THE RETURN OF RAPIDO CLINT AND MR. J.G. REEDER, *and* RAPIDO CLINT STRIKES BACK.

1b.   *Brad Counter's activities are described in Part Eleven, "Preventive Law Enforcement,"* J.T.'S HUNDREDTH, *and the Rockabye County series, covering aspects of law enforcement in present-day Texas.*

1c.   *Some of James Gunn's life story is told in Part Twelve, "The Mchawi's Powers,"* J.T.'S HUNDREDTH, *and the Bunduki series. His nickname arose from the Swahili word for a handheld firearm of any kind,* bunduki, *and gave rise to the horrible pun that when he was a child he was "Toto ya Bunduki," meaning "son of a gun."*

2.   *One occasion is recorded in* THE SOUTH WILL RISE AGAIN.

3.   *The incident is described in* BEGUINAGE.

4.   *The* Manual of Dress Regulations *for the Confederate States Army stipulated that the tunic should have "a skirt extending half way between hip and knee."*

5.   *The legacy also caused two attempts to be made on Mark's life. See* CUT ONE, THEY ALL BLEED *and Part Two, "We Hang Horse Thieves High,"* J.T.'S HUNDREDTH.

6. *"Right bower": second in command, derived from the name given to the second-highest trump card in the game of euchre.*

7. *Told in* RANGELAND HERCULES.

8. *Told in* THE MAN FROM TEXAS, *this is a rather "pin the tail on the donkey" title used by our first publishers to replace our own,* ROUNDUP CAPTAIN, *which we considered far more apt.*

9. *Evidence of Mark Counter's competence as a gunfighter and his standing compared to Dusty Fog is given in* GUN WIZARD.

10. *Martha "Calamity Jane" Canary's meetings with Mark Counter are described in Part One, "The Bounty on Belle Starr's Scalp,"* TROUBLED RANGE; *its "expansion,"* CALAMITY, MARK AND BELLE; *Part One, "Better Than Calamity,"* THE WILDCATS; *its "expansion,"* CUT ONE, THEY ALL BLEED; THE BAD BUNCH; THE FORTUNE HUNTERS; THE BIG HUNT; *and* GUNS IN THE NIGHT.

10a. *Further details about the career of Martha Jane Canary are given in the Calamity Jane series; also Part Seven, "Deadwood, August the 2nd, 1876,"* J.T.'S HUNDREDTH; *Part Six, "Mrs. Wild Bill,"* J.T.'S LADIES; *and Part Four, "Draw Poker's Such a Simple Game,"* J.T.'S LADIES RIDE AGAIN, *in which she "costars" with Belle Starr, q.v. She makes a "guest" appearance in Part Two, "A Wife for Dusty Fog,"* THE SMALL TEXAN.

11. *How Mark Counter's romance with Belle Starr commenced, progressed, and ended is told in Part One, "The Bounty on Belle Starr's Scalp,"* TROUBLED RANGE; *its "expansion,"* TEXAS TRIO; THE BAD BUNCH; RANGELAND HERCULES; THE CODE OF DUSTY FOG; *Part Two, "We Hang Horse Thieves High,"* J.T.'S HUN-

DREDTH; THE GENTLE GIANT; *Part Four,* "*A Lady Known as Belle,*" THE HARD RIDERS; *its "expansion,"* JESSE JAMES'S LOOT; *and* GUNS IN THE NIGHT.

11a. *Belle Starr "stars" no pun intended in* CARDS AND COLTS; *Part Four, "Draw Poker's Such a Simple Game,"* J.T.'S LADIES RIDE AGAIN; *and* WANTED! BELLE STARR.

11b. *Belle also makes "guest" appearances in* THE QUEST FOR BOWIE'S BLADE; *Part One, "The Set-Up,"* SAGEBRUSH SLEUTH; *its "expansion,"* WACO'S BADGE; *and Part Six, "Mrs. Wild Bill,"* J.T.'S LADIES.

11c. *We are frequently asked why it is that the "Belle Starr" we describe is so different from a photograph that appears in various books. The researches of the world's foremost fictionist genealogist, Philip Jose Farmer author of, among numerous other works,* TARZAN ALIVE, A Definitive Biography of Lord Greystoke *and* DOC SAVAGE, His Apocalyptic Life *with whom we consulted have established that the lady about whom we are writing is not the same person as another, equally famous, bearer of the name. However, the present-day members of the Counter family who supply us with information have asked Mr. Farmer and ourselves to keep her true identity a secret, and this we intend to do.*

12. *Told in* GOODNIGHT'S DREAM *and* FROM HIDE AND HORN.

13. *This is established by inference in Case Three, "The Deadly Ghost,"* YOU'RE A TEXAS RANGER, ALVIN FOG.

14. *See* IVANHOE, *by Sir Walter Scott.*

15. "Cave Adsum": *roughly translated from Latin as* "Beware, I Am Here."

16. *Information about Jessica and Trudeau Front de*

Boeuf can be found in CUT ONE, THEY ALL BLEED; *Part Three, "Responsiblity to Kinfolks,"* OLE DEVIL'S HANDS AND FEET; *and Part Four, "The Penalty of False Arrest,"* MARK COUNTER'S KIN.

Appendix Three

Raven Head, only daughter of Chief Long Walker, war leader of the Pehnane Wasp, Quick Stinger, Raider Comanche's Dog Soldier lodge and his French Creole *pairaivo*,[1] married an Irish-Kentuckian adventurer, Big Sam Ysabel, but died giving birth to their first child.

Baptized "Loncey Dalton Ysabel," the boy was raised after the fashion of the Nemenuh.[2] With his father away from the camp for much of the time, engaged upon the family's combined businesses of mustanging catching and breaking of wild horses[3] and smuggling, his education had largely been left in the hands of his maternal grandfather.[4] From Long Walker, he learned all those things a Comanche warrior must know: how to ride the wildest freshly caught mustang, or make a trained animal subservient to his will while "raiding", a polite name for the favorite pastime of the male Nemenuh, stealing horses; to follow the faintest tracks and just as effectively conceal signs of his own passing[5]; to locate hidden enemies, or keep out of sight himself when the need arose; to move in silence on the darkest of nights, or through the thickest cover; to know the ways of wild creatures[6] and, in some cases, imitate their calls so well that others of their kind were fooled.[7]

The boy proved a most excellent pupil at all the subjects. Nor were practical means of protecting himself forgotten. Not only did he learn to use all the traditional weapons of the Comanche,[8] when he had come into the possession of firearms, he had inherited his father's Kentuckian skill at shooting with a rifle and, while not real fast on the draw taking slightly over a second to bring his Colt Second Model of 1848 Dragoon revolver up and fire, whereas a tophand could practically halve that time he could perform passably with it. Furthermore, he won his Nemenuh "man-name," Cuchilo, Spanish for "Knife," by his exceptional ability at wielding one. In fact, it was claimed by those best qualified to judge that he could equal the alleged designer in performing with the massive and special type of blade that bore the name of Colonel James Bowie.[9]

Joining his father in smuggling expeditions along the Rio Grande, the boy became known to the Mexicans of the border country as *Cabrito* the Spanish name for a young goat a nickname that arose out of hearing white men refer to him as the "Ysabel Kid," but it was spoken very respectfully in that context. Smuggling was not an occupation to attract the meek and mild of manner, yet even the roughest and toughest of the bloody border's denizens came to acknowledge that it did not pay to rile up Big Sam Ysabel's son. The education received by the Kid had not been calculated to develop any overinflated belief in the sanctity of human life. When crossed he dealt with the situation like a Pehnane Dog Soldier to which war lodge of savage and most efficient warriors he had earned initiation swiftly and in an effectively deadly manner.

During the War Between the States, the Kid and his father had commenced by riding as scouts for Colonel John Singleton "the Gray Ghost" Mosby. Soon, however, their specialized knowledge and talents were diverted to having them collect and deliver to the Confederate States authorities in Texas supplies that had been purchased in Mexico, or run through the blockade by the United States Navy into Matamoros. It was hard and dangerous work,[10] but never more so than the two occasions when they became engaged in assignments with Belle "the Rebel Spy" Boyd.[11]

Soon after the War ended, Sam Ysabel was murdered. While hunting down the killers, the Kid met Captain Dustine Edward Marsden "Dusty" Fog and Mark Counter. When the mission upon which they were engaged was brought to its successful conclusion, learning the Kid no longer wished to go on either smuggling or mustanging, the small Texan offered him employment at the OD Connected ranch. It had been in the capacity as scout rather than ordinary cowhand that he was required, and his talents in that field were frequently of the greatest use as a member of the floating outfit.

The acceptance of the job by the Kid was of the greatest benefit all around. Dusty acquired another loyal friend who was ready to stick with him through any kind of peril. The ranch obtained the services of an extremely capable and efficient fighting man. For his part, the Kid was turned from a life of petty crime with the ever-present danger of having his illicit activities develop into serious law-breaking and became a useful and law-abiding member of society. Peace officers and honest citizens might have found cause to feel grateful for that. His Nemenuh upbringing would have made him a terrible and murderous outlaw if he had been driven into a life of violent crime.

Obtaining his first repeating rifle a Winchester Model of 1866, although known at that time as the "New Improved Henry," nicknamed the "Old Yellowboy" because of its brass frame while in Mexico with Dusty and Mark, the Kid had soon become an expert in its use. At the First Cochise County Fair in Arizona, despite circumstances compelling him to use a weapon with which he was not familiar,[12] he won the first prize in the rifle-shooting competition against stiff opposition. The prize was one of the legendary Winchester Model of 1873 rifles that qualified for the honored designation "One of a Thousand."[13]

It was, in part, through the efforts of the Kid that the majority of the Comanche bands agreed to go on the reservation, following attempts to ruin the signing of the treaty.[14] It was to a large extent due to his efforts that the outlaw town of Hell was located and destroyed.[15] Aided by Annie "Is-A-Man" Singing Bear a girl of mixed parentage who gained the distinction of becoming accepted as a Nemenuh warrior[16] he played a major part in preventing the attempted theft of Morton Lewis's ranch from provoking trouble with the Kweharehnuh Comanche.[17] To help a young man out of difficulties caused by a gang of card cheats, he teamed up with the lady outlaw, Belle Starr.[18] When he accompanied Martha

"Calamity Jane," Canary to inspect a ranch she had inherited, they became involved in as dangerous a situation as either had ever faced.[19]

Remaining at the OD Connected ranch until he, Dusty, and Mark met their deaths while on a hunting trip to Kenya shortly after the turn of the century, his descendants continued to be associated with the Hardin, Fog, and Blaze clan and the Counter family.[20]

1.   Pairaivo: *first, or favorite, wife. As is the case with the other Comanche terms, this is a phonetic spelling.*

2.   Nemenuh: *"the People," the Comanches' name for themselves and their nation. Members of other tribes with whom they came into contact called them, frequently with good cause, the "Tshaoh," the "Enemy People."*

3.   *A description of the way in which mustangers operated is given in* .44 CALIBRE MAN *and* A HORSE CALLED MOGOLLON.

4.   *Told in* COMANCHE.

5.   *An example of how the Ysabel Kid could conceal his tracks is given in Part One, "The Half Breed,"* THE HALF BREED *and its "expansion,"* WHITE INDIANS.

6.   *Two examples of how the Ysabel Kid's knowledge of wild animals was turned to good use are given in* OLD MOCCASINS ON THE TRAIL *and* BUFFALO ARE COMING!

7.   *An example of how well the Ysabel Kid could impersonate the call of a wild animal is recorded in Part Three, "A Wolf's a Knowing Critter,"* J.T.'S HUNDREDTH.

8.   *One occasion when the Ysabel Kid employed his skill with traditional Comanche weapons is described in* RIO GUNS.

9. *Some researchers claim that the actual designer of the knife that became permanently attached to Colonel James Bowie's name was his oldest brother, Rezin Pleasant. Although it is generally conceded that the maker was James Black, a master cutler in Arkansas, some authorities state it was manufactured by Jesse Cliffe, a white blacksmith employed by the Bowie family on their plantation in Rapides Parish, Louisiana.*

9a. *What happened to James Bowie's knife after his death in the final assault of the siege of the Alamo Mission, San Antonio de Bexar, Texas, on March 6, 1836, is told in* GET URREA *and* THE QUEST FOR BOWIE'S BLADE.

9b. *Since all of James Black's knives were custom made, there were variations in their dimensions. The specimen owned by the Ysabel Kid had a blade eleven and a half inches in length, two and a half inches wide, and a quarter of an inch thick at the guard. According to William "Bo" Randall, of Randall-Made Knives, Orlando, Florida a master cutler and authority on the subject in his own right James Bowie's knife weighed forty-three ounces, having a blade eleven inches long, two and a quarter inches wide, and three-eighths of an inch thick. His company's Model 12 "Smithsonian" Bowie knife one of which is owned by James Allenvale "Bunduki" Gunn, q.v., details of whose career can be found in the Bunduki series is modeled on it.*

9c. *One thing all "bowie" knives have in common, regardless of dimensions, is a "clip" point. The otherwise unsharpened "back" of the blade joins and becomes an extension of the main cutting surface in a concave arc, whereas a "spear" point which is less utilitarian is formed by the two sides coming together in symmetrical curves.*

10. *An occasion when Big Sam Ysabel went on a mission without his son is recorded in* THE DEVIL GUN.

11. *Told in* BLOODY BORDER *and* RENEGADE.

12. *The circumstances are described in* GUN WIZARD.

13. *When manufacturing the extremely popular Winchester Model of 1873 rifle which they claimed to be the "Gun Which Won the West" the makers selected all those barrels found to shoot with exceptional accuracy to be fitted with set triggers and given a special fine finish. Originally, these were inscribed "1 of 1,000," but this was later changed to script: "One of a Thousand." However, the title was a considerable understatement. Only 136 out of a total production of 720,610 qualified for the distinction. Those of a grade lower were to be designated "One of a Hundred," but only seven were so named. The practice commenced in 1875 and was discontinued three years later because the management decided it was not good sales policy to suggest that different grades of gun were being produced.*

14. *Told in* SIDEWINDER.

15. *Told in* HELL IN THE PALO DURO *and* GO BACK TO HELL.

16. *How Annie Singing Bear acquired the distinction of becoming a warrior and won her "man-name" is told in* IS-A-MAN.

17. *Told in* WHITE INDIANS.

18. *Told in Part Two, "The Poison and the Cure,"* WANTED! BELLE STARR.

19. *Told in* WHITE STALLION, RED MARE.

20. *Mark Scrapton, a grandson of the Ysabel Kid, served as a member of Company "Z," Texas Rangers, with Alvin Dustine "Cap" Fog and Ranse Smith respectively, grandson of Captain Dustine Edward Marsden "Dusty" Fog and Mark Counter during the Prohibition era. Information about their specialized duties is recorded in the Alvin Dustine "Cap" Fog series.*

223

If you have enjoyed reading this large print book and you would like more information on how to order a Wheeler Large Print Book, please write to:

 Wheeler Publishing, Inc.
P.O. Box 531
Accord, MA 02018-0531